RODEO KILLER

RODEO KILLER

by

Derek Taylor

Dales Large Print Books
Long Preston, North Yorkshire,
BD23 4ND, England.

British Library Cataloguing in Publication Data.

Taylor, Derek
   Rodeo killer.

   A catalogue record of this book is
   available from the British Library

   ISBN   1-84262-186-6 pbk

First published in Great Britain 2001 by Robert Hale Limited

Copyright © Derek Taylor 2001   WES
                                      1426641

Cover illustration © Longarron by arrangement with
Norma Editorial

Published in Large Print 2002 by arrangement with
Robert Hale Limited

Dales Large Print is an imprint of Library Magna Books Ltd.

Printed and bound in Great Britain by
T.J. (International) Ltd., Cornwall, PL28 8RW

For Alice and Jim Niven in Texas for kindly showing me the ropes.

ONE

It was the hottest Fourth of July in living memory. People would have preferred to stay in the shade. But it was the fourth of July and that meant rodeo.

'Red, you gonna ride a bull for sure?' his kid brother asked.

'Sure am, Jimboy, and ain't no one gonna stop me. Least of all them dudes over at Five Rings.'

Jimboy was silent for a moment, contemplating the risk his reckless brother was aiming to take. But he couldn't stop him. Never mind that Hal Turner had threatened violence, if Red entered the bull-riding this year, claiming that it was Red's fault that his brother had been gored to death last year as he was about to win the title.

'You ain't fretting none about Hal

9

Turner's threats, are you?' Red asked Jimboy. Jimboy's look answered his question. 'Hal's a big mouth,' Red continued, 'who's too yella to try anything. If he weren't, he'd be riding a bull this afternoon, trying to beat me the way Lee did.'

'No, but look who he has got riding for the Five Rings.'

Red realized nothing he could say would reassure his brother and he decided to let the matter drop.

'Hey, Jimbo,' he suddenly declared. 'I gotta get me warmed up. Let's go ride out for a while. I'll race yer to Murphy's Springs!'

While Red Arnold was fine-tuning his athletic prowess, Hal Turner was already at the rodeo site, an open flat near the courthouse in Pecos, Texas. The year was 1891. He'd already consumed a lot of beer and was full enough of bravado to be shooting off his mouth about what he was going to do to Red Arnold if he dared to show up at the rodeo with Lucy Phillips, the girl he'd stolen from his elder brother Lee the day before he was killed in last year's rodeo.

'Maybe we should make sure he don't get here at all,' one of his bosom pals suggested.

'Yeh, let's go and blow him away on the trail,' uttered another of his pals, Joey Sands, a little runt of a cowboy who wanted the world to think he was tall and tough. 'And I'll pull the trigger.'

Hal Turner looked around. The saloon was full of people, mainly cowboys getting ready for the rodeo. He hadn't formulated in his mind any plan for dealing with Red Arnold should he show. He'd just put out the word that there'd be trouble if he did. But what trouble could he make in a crowd of people whose darling Red was for being a regular sort of guy and for being Deer County's champion bull-rider? Maybe it wasn't such a bad idea after all to get him before he arrived in town. That way no one could prevent him from making sure Red never got to go anywhere near a bull in this year's rodeo.

Without saying too much, he got up from his seat and simply walked out of the saloon. The others didn't ask where he was going, but just followed him. He was about to swing up on his horse, when a voice called out.

'Where you going, Hal? Thought you was here for the rodeo?' It was the town sheriff.

Turner stopped dead in his tracks, taking his foot out of the stirrup.

'Hi, there, Sheriff. I was just fixing to take the boys here for a ride. You know, get them loosened up a bit for the rodeo,' he answered the sheriff, thinking quick.

'Are you sure that's all you're aiming to do?' the sheriff, whose name was Delaney, asked.

He knew Hal Turner of old and had reckoned he'd better be on the look-out for trouble. Turner's threats had reached just about everyone in town who might have an interest in knowing of them.

'Yeah, what else?' Joey replied in a goofy sort of way that made Turner feel like clipping his ear. Instead he threw him the kind of look that told him to shut up, if he knew what was good for him. The others already knew better than to speak when not spoken to.

'Ain't against the law to take a ride now, is it, Sheriff?' was Turner's reply to Sheriff Delaney.

'Not unless you got trouble-making on your mind?'

'And why would I have?' Turner replied, a defiant look in his eye.

'Don't play games with me, sonny boy,' replied Sheriff Delaney, who was old enough to be Turner's father, and some. 'Now I'm telling you this once and once only. You make any trouble between you and Red Arnold and I'll have you in that jailhouse,' he pointed in the direction of his office, 'quicker than a bull can throw you. Is that understood?'

Turner did not like being told what's what in front of his gang but the only reply he dared throw the famously no-nonsense town sheriff was a look of dumb insolence. This was enough to tell the sheriff that he'd got the message and he was prepared to leave it at that. He'd long since learned you had to leave a bad guy at least some small face-saving, if you wanted to give him the opportunity to walk away from trouble.

'Right, then,' the sheriff concluded, putting his hand on his gun and turning to walk away, eyeballing Turner to the last.

Watching him go, Turner was unsure of what to do next. Then he made up his mind. 'All right,' he said. 'There's time enough yet to take care of Arnold.' And with that he led his gang back to the saloon, pushing Joey ahead of him in a belittling kind of way.

TWO

By the time Red and Jimboy Arnold rode into town the rodeo was in full swing. Pecos's two saloons were full of cowboys making a riotous time of it, while the family men were picnicking with their families close to the makeshift arena which had been constructed near to the courthouse. Red and Jimboy rode into town just in time to witness the first fracas of the day. They were tying up their horses and it was just gone midday.

'I ain't chicken and I'll kill anyone who says I am!' a cowboy was heard to shout as he came bounding out of a saloon with his sixgun drawn.

'Just calm down, Mickey,' another man who was trying to restrain his right arm was saying.

Just then a shot rang out from within the

saloon and Mickey's hat flew from his head.

'Why, that son of a gun!' the cowboy snarled, pushing his sidekick from him and firing off a number of shots into the saloon.

Sheriff Delaney, who was at the other end of the small town, heard the shots and dropped what he was doing to come and investigate.

'That's Mickey, ain't it?' Jimboy declared.

'It sure is,' replied Red, 'and he's gonna get himself killed if he ain't careful.'

Mickey was one of the Arnolds' circle of friends. He'd broken a leg badly being thrown from a bronc a few years before and it had left him with a severe limp. He was still standing on the plankwalk in front of the saloon. Bullets coming from inside the saloon were zinging past him, but incredibly none had hit him. Red decided he had to do something before something fatal happened to him. Without pausing to consider the danger to himself, he threw himself at Mickey and brought him down on the boardwalk in front of the saloon's batwing doors and out of any immediate danger. Before either of them could collect themselves, the cowboy who'd been firing the shots that had come from inside the saloon came striding through the batwing doors on to the boardwalk outside the saloon. He was ready to shoot to kill but when he saw Red and Mickey lying in a heap he hesitated, not wanting to hit the wrong man.

'Put it up.' It was Jimboy. He'd drawn his own sixgun and was now pointing it menacingly at the cowboy. Hardly had the words issued from his mouth when the cowboy turned on his heels, his free hand going like lightning to fan the trigger of his Colt .45. But he was not quick enough for Jimboy, who, having already cocked his gun, had only to pull the trigger. The bullet he fired slapped dead centre of the cowboy's guts and sent him slamming into the batwing doors and back into the saloon.

'Thanks, Jimbo,' Red said disentangling himself from Mickey and getting to his feet.

Mickey was about to offer up his thanks

when Sheriff Delaney suddenly appeared amongst them.

'What'n glory's name has been going on here?' he asked.

Before anyone could answer him Hal Turner came striding out of the saloon. He was looking to avenge the cowboy's death but was stopped in his tracks by the sight of Delaney standing there.

'I shot in self-defence, Sheriff, as Red and Mickey here will tell yer,' Jimboy declared.

'I know,' replied the sheriff, 'that much I saw. But who started it?'

Before either of the Arnolds or Mickey could say anything Turner pointed a finger at Mickey, implying that it had all been his fault, saying, 'Mickey fired the first shot.'

'Let me look at your gun,' Delaney said to Mickey, who drew his Colt .45 and handed it to him.

The sheriff sniffed the barrel and opened the chamber. Nothing told him the gun had been used that day, let alone in the last few minutes.

'It don't appear to me you're telling the truth here, Turner.'

Turner began to argue the case but Delaney shut him up, saying, 'Turner, wherever you turn up trouble soon follows. Now unless you want to sit out the rest of the day in the cell block, I suggest you pipe down some and get back to your own affairs.'

Looking meaner than ever, Turner idly about-turned and walked back into the saloon. But not before the look in his eye told Red Arnold that the matter wasn't over yet. Delaney watched him go, then he turned to the Arnold boys and Mickey and said, 'All right, now, I don't want no more trouble from you three today either, or you'll end up in the cells alongside him. Now go find the undertaker and tell him he's needed.'

And with that he turned and followed Turner into the saloon. A man had been killed but in Pecos it was nothing so out of the ordinary. It was Jimboy's first killing and a range of emotions was filling both him and Red, but they didn't show it. In the Wild West a man's baptism was usually a baptism of fire.

Back in the saloon Hal Turner was letting off steam, even as he watched the sheriff and the town undertaker remove the dead cowboy's body. Turner's threats, though, got lost in the general din of the Fourth of July revelling that was going on. But what was clear to Joey and the other members of his gang was that Turner was not going to rest that day until Red Arnold was well and truly sorted for the wrong they all reckoned had been done to his brother at last year's Fourth of July rodeo.

'Come on,' Turner suddenly declared, slamming his empty beer-glass down on the counter. 'Bronc riding'll be starting soon. Let's see which one of you sons of bitches stays on the longest.'

The first one up was Sharky Caldwell on a wild bucker called Webfoot, so-called because he had such big, heavy looking hoofs. People gasped as despite Webfoot's determined efforts to unseat his rider, Sharky Caldwell managed to hang on for more than just a few minutes. In those early days when there was no limit set on how long a cowboy could be expected to remain in place, either on a bull or a bronco horse, anything above sixty seconds was considered impressive enough. Joey Sands only managed to stay on for two, but he was admired for having a go and was pleased enough with his performance. Hal Turner, though, despite the beer he'd consumed, or maybe because of it, rode his bronc for more than three minutes. Nobody had seen a horse pitch and buck with such determination, arching its back and jumping so high it looked like it'd never come down. But still Turner hung on, even when his horse's hind legs kicked so high it seemed he made an angle of ninety degrees with the ground.

Red Arnold saw him do it and couldn't

help but be mightily impressed. He never rode broncs himself, preferring to stick to bulls.

'He's got it. No one'll beat that!' Jimboy called into his ear.

'No,' Red agreed, remembering the one person who would have done. Turner's brother, Lee. Hal was competent enough and could stay on a bucking horse long enough to make a good showing of it, but his brother had been an all round rodeo champion, riding both broncs and bulls. Added to which he was the sort of nice guy that everyone liked. As Red's mind filled with the memory of what happened last year, when he saw Lee gored to death, he felt sick in the pit of his stomach. But then someone touched his arm. He turned to find it was Lucy, formerly Lee's girlfriend, that is, before she had become his own.

'Why, Lucy, honey!' he exclaimed. 'You're here. I looked for you earlier but couldn't find you.'

'We broke a wheel on the buggy and got

here late.'

'Is that so? Nobody hurt, I hope,' Red said, wanting to take her in his arms but not daring to in front of all the people gathered to watch the rodeo events.

Suddenly a gasp of horror went up from the crowd. Turning back to face the bronc riding, Red saw why. Turner had been thrown but he got to his feet without a second's delay and the crowd's collected gasp turned to relief and a harmonious cheer that was loud enough to be heard all over town. Red did not add his own voice to the crowd's expression of delight, but instead turned and walked away, indicating to Lucy and Jimboy that they should follow him.

'He's good, ain't he?' remarked Jimboy. 'You gotta give him that. Even if Lee was better.'

As he said it Jimboy wished he hadn't. Any mention of Lee's name was an embarrassment to Lucy and Tom and he could have kicked himself for being so thoughtless.

'Come on,' he quickly said to his brother, wanting to change the subject as quickly as he'd introduced it, 'we gotta get ready for the bull-riding.'

'Just come and say hello to Mamma first,' Lucy said to Red. 'She'll be hurt if you don't, you know that.'

'Of course, I will,' was Red's reply. Turning to his brother, he added, 'You go, Jimbo. I'll be there in a minute.'

'Well, don't be long,' Jimboy replied, turning to go. 'They'll be drawing the bulls soon. And if you ain't there when they do so, you won't get a ride.'

'All right.' Red smiled affectionately at his younger brother. 'Don't worry, I'll be there.'

Lucy's family were very fond of Red, her mother especially, and they greeted him warmly.

'I was afraid I was gonna miss seeing you ride,' her father said to him.

'Why,' said her mother, 'we ain't even had time to eat our picnic!'

'Come along, son,' Lucy's father declared,

looking over at the arena, 'looks to me like the bronc riding's over and the bull-riding'll be starting soon.'

Red was no bronc-rider but he could ride a bull and after Lee Turner was the best the Pecos Fourth of July Rodeo had seen.

'That's all right, Red,' Lucy's mother declared. 'You run along. By the time you've finished your ride, Lucy and I will have the picnic laid out and you can join us to eat.'

Red knew that Lucy would not be coming to watch him ride. It wasn't the done thing. Her father surely would, though. Clapping an arm around his shoulders he walked him to the arena. Red's own parents were still in Midland, there to attend his maternal grandmother's funeral. Red and Jimboy had stayed behind to look after the ranch and compete in the one event of the year no young buck ever wanted to miss, the rodeo.

At the arena's side near where the officials had their tables, Hal Turner's gang were gathered around him congratulating him on his winning ride. Turner saw Red coming with Lucy's father and it filled him with anger.

'Look at that,' he sneered, causing Joey Sands and the others to suddenly go quiet and look to see what he was talking about. When they saw Red approaching they soon guessed.

'That should be Lee,' Joey remarked, 'walking with Mr Phillips's arm around his shoulders, coming to make the best ride.'

'You said it,' was all Turner uttered by way of a reply to Joey's words. 'You said it.'

Red and Lucy's father simply walked on past to where the bulls were being drawn. As they passed him, Red kept his eyes turned away from Turner's. Lucy's father didn't, instead throwing his way a cordial enough greeting. He'd heard of the threats Turner was making and was none too impressed by them.

'What you gonna do, Hal?' Joey asked.

'Shut up, Joey!' Turner snapped in reply. Turning to the others, he simply asked, 'Who's got my rifle?'

THREE

Red's turn came to ride his bull. He'd drawn one of the fiercest on offer, a black Brahma called Outlaw Willie. If bronc-riding is thrilling, bull riding takes your breath away. Men ride horses and everyone is familiar with that. A bronc could be seen as just a wild, manic mount that needs taming; but a bull, with all its porterhouse bulk and threatening demeanour, well, who in his right mind would want to get up on one and ride something so obviously not made for it? And what a champion would be the man who stayed on the longest? And 'longest' in the early days of the rodeo meant just that. Nowadays a cowboy is only expected to stay on a maximum of eight seconds but in those days to beat an opponent it could take as long as four minutes.

27

Lee Turner had broken all the records at Pecos by staying on nearly five and it had made him a super-hero amongst all his friends and admirers. Then had come along Red Arnold, not only to challenge Lee's position as number one bull-rider but also to steal his girl. Lucy, the most beautiful girl in the county, always maintained she had never considered herself Lee Turner's girl; she hadn't felt herself ready yet to become anyone's girl. Lee had made certain assumptions but in doing so he had jumped the gun and she'd told him so. But with Red it had been something different. For both of them it had been love at first sight. It was as straightforward as that but it made Lee feel as if he had been dumped at the altar and it filled him with bitterness. Last Fourth of July it had taken his mind off his bull-riding and made it a very dangerous sport for him to indulge in. For weeks before the rodeo he had not even bothered to practise. It hadn't altered his ability to stay on the bull longer than anyone else, but it had dented his ability to get away from the raging, two-ton shovel on four feet fast enough. In the end it had cost him his life. Hal Turner blamed this on the fact that the day before the rodeo Lucy and Red had announced their engagement and he hated Lucy for it. But you couldn't punish a woman. With Red, though, it was a different matter. And Red was going to pay. That was a certainty. Lee had won the bull-riding prize last year, even though it had been given to him posthumously; Red, his only serious challenger, was not going to be allowed to walk away with it this year, especially not to share it with that two timing Jezebel, Lucy Phillips.

Red was on his bull, the rope had been tightened and the fingers of his left hand were wrapped firmly around the handgrip. Suddenly the bull was let loose and Red was hanging on for dear life. Outlaw Willie with fleet nimbleness spun to the left and then to the right. Red had barely shifted his centre of gravity to cope with this, when he dropped his head down and threw his hind legs. Red hung on, his free hand held high above his head, his left arm feeling as if it was about to be wrenched from its elbow socket. The crowd gasped, none of them believing that he could stay on the straining steer's back a second longer. The aim that Hal Turner was taking would make sure he didn't. He was on top of the courthouse, a three-storey building that gave him a perfect line of fire. A lot of shots were being fired off in the saloons on Main Street and no one paid any attention to the crack Turner's rifle made as he pulled the trigger. The spectators watching the bull-ride saw Red fall but all assumed it was because the bull had at last thrown him. It wasn't long though, before they realized something was wrong. Blood appeared on the front of Red's shirt and he lay on the ground not moving. But for one of the clowns, men whose job it was to distract the bull and stop it attacking its unseated tormentor before he could get away, Red would have been gored or at least tossed around the arena as if he were a rag doll. Just as Lee Turner had been last year.

As Outlaw Willie was driven off and penned, the arena officials began to wonder what had happened. Red Arnold lay on the ground and was not moving.

'He's been shot!' his brother exclaimed as he lifted him and rested his shoulders on his knees. At first he thought he'd been killed but much to his relief Red suddenly began to utter a few words. 'He's alive,' he exclaimed, his voice full of relief. 'Call the doctor, somebody, call the doctor.'

Hal Turner watched from the courthouse roof, his gang around him.

'Dang, I don't know if I killed him or not. I should have gotten in a second shot while I could.'

'We'd better get out of here, Hal,' one of the gang said, 'before someone guesses where the shot came from.'

Seeing the sense of what had been suggested, Turner began to make tracks. But not before looking back towards the arena,

31

wondering if there was any possibility he could get off one more shot at Red Arnold. But it was useless. Red couldn't be seen now for the people who crowded around him. One of them was Sheriff Delaney. Turner and his gang disappeared from sight as the sheriff turned to study where the shot might have come from.

'It was Turner,' Jimboy informed him. 'Must have been. Can't have been nobody else.'

'You reckon?' was all Sheriff Delaney said to him, for he'd begun to walk away, his gaze fixed now on the courthouse.

Red was by now fully conscious and trying to get to his feet. The doctor considered it was safe enough to let him and Jimboy helped him walk out of the arena.

'Better come straight to my surgery, Red,' the doctor advised him. 'There's a bullet lodged in that shoulder and the sooner it comes out the better.'

As people made way for him, talking with one another and trying to make sense of what had happened, Lucy suddenly appeared pushing her way through them.

'My God, Red!' she exclaimed on seeing him. 'What happened?'

So busy and bustling was the day, she had not heard the shot, nor known that anything had happened until someone ran and told her. Jumping up and without leave of her parents, she'd rushed immediately to be at Red's side. Turner came round from the back of the courthouse and joined the crowds just in time to see her go. It filled him with a sour indignation and made him wish again his shot had been fatal. As Lucy ran towards the crush of people filling the arena, he turned and ambled towards Mason's Saloon, the drinking establishment he frequented most when in Pecos. Bitch! he thought to himself. Next time you *will* be turned into a widow, you can count on that.

Later that evening his stomping and cavorting shook the puncheon-floor of the saloon as he danced a Cotton-eyed Joe to a local string-band led by champion fiddle-player Bob Wills. While just a few blocks away Red Arnold lay sweating in a fever caused by the bullet-wound in his shoulder becoming infected. The doctor said he had been a very lucky young man. Another inch or two, to the left or the right, and he'd have died. Lucy had got permission from her parents to remain at his side. Jimboy had stayed there too, ordered to do so by Sheriff Delaney, who'd feared he might go seeking revenge against the man he'd insisted he knew had shot his brother.

'Sheriff, are you gonna arrest him or what?' Jimboy asked Sheriff Delaney as he turned to leave the doctor's surgery.

'I gotta make a few enquiries first, son.'

'I know he did it,' Jimboy insisted again as he had been doing since Delaney first appeared on the scene after Red Arnold had been shot.

'It ain't as simple as your knowing. I gotta be able to prove it. Now, you just look after your brother and leave me to do my job,' the sheriff replied. 'If Hal Turner did do it, he'll pay, you don't have to worry none about that.'

'I wish Ma and Pa was here,' Jimboy opined, turning back to look down at his brother, whose fevered brow was being tenderly mopped with a cold flannel held in Lucy's tender loving hand.

'Yeah,' was all the sheriff said, laying an avuncular and comforting hand on Jimboy's shoulder before turning and leaving the doctor's surgery.

Sheriff Delaney had already made a number of enquiries but on all of them he'd drawn a blank. No one had seen Hal Turner, or anyone for that matter, fire on Red Arnold. To nail Hal Turner he had to have proof, even if there simply wasn't anyone else on whom suspicion might fall. He knew where Turner was hanging out and decided he'd pay the place a visit.

The town was still full of people having a good time, only now they were mostly to be found in the saloons. Delaney had a brace of deputies keeping an eye on things and he wasn't really expecting more than the usual rowdyism. He found Mason's to be fairly rocking. Bob Wills and his band had not let up and the drink had loosened everyone's limbs. Wills saw Delaney come through the batwing doors and had thrown him one of his irresistibly charismatic smiles. Trouble was never heard of at a Bob Wills dance, the man's presence somehow or other just didn't facilitate it. Smiling back, Delaney pushed his way through the crowd to the bar.

'Evening, Sheriff,' the barkeep called over the din. 'Your usual?'

Knocking it back a few minutes later, Delaney cast his eye about the saloon until it fell upon Turner. He was sitting at a table surrounded by his gang. One of them had walked away with the bronc champion's prize, a hundred dollars and a cup. There wasn't a great deal of the money left but the cup held pride of place in the middle of the table. It was obvious to Delaney that Turner and his gang were full of themselves. Well, you'd expect them to be, he was thinking to himself, when suddenly Joey got to his feet and drank a toast.

'Here's to Red Arnold and that bullet you put in him!' he sang out, raising his beer-glass high.

What Joey lacked in size he made up for with his voice. It carried across the floor to the sheriff's ears. It only confirmed what he already knew. Delaney, though, was not about to wade in to a drunken crowd to do anything about it. It would have to wait until later, when Turner and his cohorts were making their drunken way to the cowboys' dime-a-night Bunkhouse Hotel.

Someone for whom it could not wait, though, was Mickey, the Arnold brothers' friend. He'd been watching Turner all evening, his bitterness at what had happened to Red growing deeper and deeper the more beer he drank. The friends he was with had restrained him, though, and he'd done nothing more than keep an eagle eye on

Turner and his gang. But hearing Joey's toast made his blood boil. He'd been leaning with his back against the bar supported by his elbows. Standing up straight, and pushing his belt and holster down firmly into place, he began to take the few steps needed to bring him to Turner's table.

As he got closer to the table he began to push people out of his way. But before any of them could properly find out what was going on Mickey had leapt on to Turner and pushed him from his chair on to the floor. As Turner's men jumped up from their seats intending to rush to his aid they were suddenly set upon by friends of Mickey's and the Arnolds.

It wasn't long before a stray punch caught the wrong target and a general fracas erupted. Soon everyone was punching everyone. Bottles and chairs began to fly. Bob Wills ordered his band to play on. Sheriff Delaney began to call for order and would have drawn his gun to sound a few warning shots had a chair not hit him across the shoulders and sent him sprawling.

Mickey's fists had pounded into Turner's face but he was now getting the worst of it. He reached for his gun but someone knocked it out of his hand. Then someone else hit him over the head with a whiskey bottle and he fell to the ground. Turner, collecting himself quickly, picked up a chair and broke it over him. He was about to kick Mickey in the head when shots rang out. It brought him and everyone else to their senses.

Delaney's two deputies were standing just inside the batwing doors with their guns still smoking. Getting to his feet, Sheriff Delaney took charge of things.

'Arrest Mickey Slater and Hal Turner,' he barked at one of his deputies. He was still not steady on his feet and pushed his way to the bar to steady himself against it.

'What for?' he heard Turner indignantly demanding of the deputy who'd been instructed to arrest him. 'It was Mickey here who started it. Why arrest me?'

'Come on,' was all the deputy said in reply, making menacing gestures with his gun. Turner realized he had no choice but to do as he was told. His men, as they collected themselves, would at a sign from him have interfered to help him but no sign came and Turner was led away.

Mickey was still out cold on the floor. The other deputy had called for a jug of water which he threw over him. It brought Mickey round and he was ordered to get to his feet and was then taken off to the town cells. Bob Wills, who'd stopped playing when the deputies pumped shots into the ceiling, started to play again. While Sheriff Delaney, casting a threatening look around the saloon, followed his deputies out of the saloon.

'All right, all right,' he heard the voice of the owner of the saloon call out. 'Trouble's over. Let's get to clearing up.'

FOUR

The next day had many of the citizens of Pecos feeling that a tornado had visited their town. Many of them awoke with hangovers. Normally the two Arnold boys would have shared in their experience but not this year. Red's fever had not broken and Jimboy had endured a fitful night worrying about it. Lucy had barely slept at all. Seeing Red so callously wounded and then so ill, had made her realize how deeply her love for him went. She was seventeen, which in the early 90s of America's Wild West era made her well on the way to reaching her prime, and was ready for marriage and child-bearing. She wanted her husband to be Red Arnold and her children to be his. In the lonely hours before dawn she petitioned her Baptist saviour to let him live.

Hal Turner had had no trouble sleeping. The moment he was thrown into a cell and his head hit the rough cotton of the pillow on the wooden bed he fell into a drunken sleep, from which he did not awaken until gone seven the following morning.

'Who's there?' he called out loudly, after a few moments of collecting himself.

Sitting dozing at Sheriff Delaney's desk, Deputy Rogers was doing the night-shift. He was shocked into wakefulness by Turner's enquiry.

'I am,' he replied. 'Now shut your racket, Turner, before I come in there and shut it for you.'

'I need some coffee,' was Turner's reply. He reached for the makings he kept in his waistcoat pocket and started building himself a cigarette. 'Want one of these?' he asked.

Deputy Rogers, who was poking the ashes of a stove to get it hot enough to warm up some coffee, ignored him. There were a few moments silence, during which time Mickey in the cell next to Turner's stirred but didn't waken. Turner could see him through the bars that separated their cells and he suddenly became mindful of what had happened the night before to land them in custody. Lighting the cigarette he'd made, he stood up and stepped towards the front bars of his cell.

'Guess I can go now,' he remarked. 'I gotta round up the boys and get back to the ranch, otherwise my old pa will have my hide.'

Deputy Rogers' inclination was to let Turner do just that. Drunken fights on the Fourth of July were nothing new and it was the usual procedure to let anyone whose excesses had landed them in trouble go the next morning, the ignominy of spending a night in the cells being deemed punishment enough for the nuisance they'd caused. However, this time there were more serious matters to hand. A man had been shot and Hal Turner, son though he might be of the biggest rancher in those parts, was the main suspect.

'Well, that'll be up to the sheriff to decide.'

'Sheriff?' questioned Turner, insinuating by his tone of voice that the matter wasn't as serious as that.

'Yeah,' Rogers replied, handing Turner a tin mug of coffee through the bars. 'Somebody shot Red Arnold. You ain't forgotten that, have you?'

'What's it to do with me?'

The feigned tone of innocence in his voice did not impress Rogers one way or the other.

'We'll have to wait and see, won't we?' he replied, going back to the stove and pouring a mug of coffee for Mickey. 'Wake up, boy!' he sang out, stepping up to the front of Mickey's cell. 'Time you was out of here.'

Mickey stepped out of the sheriff's office on to the plank walk just in time to see Delaney approaching. He'd have preferred to avoid him but was not so lucky.

'You deserve to feel as bad as you look,' the sheriff chastised him. 'Go find your friends and get out of town before noon, or I'll arrest you all and make you pay for the

44

damage you done at Mason's last night.'

Showing genuine contriteness, Mickey was suitably respectful to the sheriff and hurried on his way. Delaney paused for barely a second to watch him go and then marched into his office. He greeted Rogers and told him he could go. Turner, who a few moments before had been remonstrating with Rogers over the what he considered to be the unjustness of letting Mickey go while keeping him in custody, turned his attention to Delaney.

'It ain't right, Sheriff, you keeping me in here, and my daddy won't like it.'

Delaney knew that what Turner said about his father was true, but it did not give him any undue cause for concern. The Turners, while being one of the richest ranching families in the county, were nevertheless a decent family. Hal was their black sheep, but his activities up until then had not been criminal, merely delinquent. It changed things, even if proving whether or not he shot Red Arnold was going to be the main

45

issue from here on.

'I think your daddy will be just as keen as I am to find out who shot Red, don't you think, Hal?' Delaney replied, going to the stove and pouring himself a mug of coffee.

Turner's air of feigned nonchalance wasn't as strong as it had been. But even so he knew no one other than his gang had seen him shoot Red Arnold and that none of them would dare give him away. What he'd forgotten about, though, was what had taken place the night before.

'What you suggesting, Sheriff?'

'It ain't what I'm suggesting,' Delaney replied, casually going to his desk and sitting down. 'It's what Joey said. Last night.'

'Joey?' queried Turner.

'Yeah. Raised his glass and drank to your health for putting that slug in Red Arnold's shoulder.'

'Joey's full of shit. You know that, Sheriff.'

'Maybe, maybe not this time. Reckon it's cause enough to put you on trial, though, don't you?'

'People say all sorts of boastful things when they're drunk. Get him here now, though, and see what he has to say.'

'One of my deputies is out bringing him in.'

'Good. Then maybe we can get this matter cleared up and I can get out of here.'

Sheriff Delaney knew Joey would be too afraid to say anything against Turner but he nevertheless had to give it a try. The crime so far was relatively minor, but if Red Arnold died, it wouldn't be. Then, he knew, he'd be dealing with a big-shot lawyer from Midland whose only purpose would be not to let a murderer walk free.

Turner spent a fretful few hours waiting for Joey to be brought in. When he was it looked to him as if he'd been roughed up some and he commented on the fact to Deputy Rogers.

'Yeah, well,' Rogers replied, 'Jimboy Arnold found him before I did.'

'But I didn't say nothing though,' Joey was quick to point out to Turner.

'Well, that don't surprise me none, since there was nothing you could say,' Turner was quick to retort.

The mean look in his eye told Joey he'd done well to keep his mouth shut.

'That's what I said, Hal, though they was going on about me boasting you had shot Red Arnold. I don't recall no such thing. Not that I recall anything much about last night.'

'So, Sheriff, you gonna let me go now or what?' Turner asked.

Sheriff Delaney's reply was not immediate. He had to think on things a bit. Turner's family was influential and the evidence they had so far was flimsy to say the least. But yet he knew Turner had shot Red Arnold and he wanted him to pay the price for it. Looking at Turner, though, he decided he had no choice but to let him go.

'All right, you can go,' he said, taking the cell keys from a drawer in his desk. 'But you make sure you go straight home. In fact, I'll take you there myself and see what your father has to say about things. No doubt word will have reached him by now of what's happened.'

Turner wasn't too pleased at the thought of being escorted home but reckoned it wasn't worth arguing about. He'd have preferred to roam the brush some before having to face the wrath of his father, but supposed that now was as good a time as any to be on the receiving end of his father's tongue-lashing.

'What about me, Sheriff?' Joey asked as Delaney pushed the key in the lock and opened Turner's cell door.

'What about you, Joey?' Delaney asked pointedly. 'That depends on whether or not your memory returns. In the meantime scram. Go on, get outa here.'

Joey didn't wait to be told twice. Without any reference to Turner, he pushed past Delaney's deputy and was gone.

'What do you think, Doctor?'

'We'll have to wait and see,' Doctor

Ritchie replied, taking Red Arnold's pulse and feeling it race. 'He's a fit young man. He should be OK.'

Red Arnold was still feverish. His bullet wound was looking angry and he was making nonsensical utterances. It frightened Lucy, who didn't have any experience of such things, and she was afraid for the life of one whom she reckoned now to be her betrothed.

'You should go home now, child,' Doctor Ritchie added, 'and get some sleep. We don't want you getting ill.'

Lucy's mother had come by and she told Lucy she agreed with the doctor.

'But Mother!' Lucy began.

'Red will be all right,' Doctor Ritchie reassured her. 'My wife will be here to nurse him.'

Mrs Ritchie, a matronly sort of woman, smiled reassuringly at Lucy, saying if there was any change in Red's condition they would send for her immediately.

'Where is Jimboy?' Lucy asked.

'He's gone back to the ranch. I saw him on my way here. He's got to take care of things there. He's sent a telegram to his parents in Midland and no doubt they'll come straight back,' Mrs Phillips replied, putting her hands gently on Lucy's shoulders to lead her away.

As she allowed herself to be led out of the doctor's surgery, Lucy looked over her shoulder at Red. He was quieter now but not really still. Suddenly breaking down, she fell against her mother, letting her tears flow for the first time since Red had been shot down.

FIVE

By railroad Midland was not so far from Pecos. Shocked and horrified by the news their younger son's telegram brought them, the Arnolds left for home immediately,

anxious to know the circumstances sur-
rounding their eldest son being shot. They
were aware of the animosity that existed
between Red and Hal Turner and Mr
Arnold feared that Red might have been
involved in a shoot-out with him.

'I always said that Turner boy was nothing
but trouble,' Mrs Arnold declared to her
husband.

But he made no reply, his thoughts running on to contemplate where a quarrel
between his and the Turners' families might
lead. Pecos was once quiet, he reflected.
Then came the railroad and hot on its tail
gun-toting opportunists and ne'er-do-wells.
He had been confident, though, that his
sons would not get caught up in it all.

Sheriff Delaney's thoughts as he rode out of
town with Hal Turner were equally reflec-
tive of what a hell-hole Pecos had become.
As they passed the doctor's surgery he
thought of poor Red Arnold lying there,
dying, for all anyone knew, and it made him

mad. Decent families had no place in the town and its environs any more. Well, it was his job to change that, and change it was what he was determined to do, regardless of what it took. Even sitting astride his horse Turner's demeanour was full of swagger. He'd gotten away with it, in his own mind he was sure of it. Well, thought Delaney, we'll see about that.

They'd gone a few miles east when they came up against riders from the Five Rings, the Turner family ranch.

'Howdy, Sheriff. We was just coming into town to see what's what,' Del Lawson, foreman of the Five Rings, greeted Delaney, before nodding his head in the direction of Hal Turner.

'What's what,' Turner sneered before the sheriff had a chance to return Lawson's greeting, 'is that they're trying to pin something on me without any proof.'

'We heard there'd been some trouble, Hal, and your daddy sent me to investigate.'

Lawson's tone was reasonable enough, but

in fact he had no time for his employer's youngest son, thinking him spoilt and difficult to control.

'Someone shot the Arnold boy while he was participating in the bull-riding yesterday and Joey Sands boasted it was Hal here,' Delaney informed Lawson.

'He was drunk, Del, and didn't know what he was saying. And anyway he now denies saying it, so, you know, what's this all about?'

Lawson studied Turner for a moment, saying nothing. He was aware of the ill-feeling that existed between him and Red Arnold over the Phillips girl and what he reckoned she had to do with his brother's death at least year's rodeo. More than likely, he concluded, he did shoot Red Arnold, but if this was all the proof they had, he couldn't see his boss taking the matter lying down.

Delaney had said nothing more. He knew he couldn't keep Turner under arrest but had thought it important to put the law's case to his father.

'You shoot Red Arnold?' Lawson suddenly asked Turner.

'Nope,' Turner lied.

'Well, I guess that's it, Sheriff. You ain't got any proof he did it and he denies it. We'll take him off your hands and take him home.'

Delaney eyeballed Lawson, trying to read in his eyes whether or not be believed Turner. If it seemed he did, then he'd accompany them back to the Five Rings to confront Turner senior. If it seemed he didn't, he'd let Turner go with him and wait to see how his father intended to deal with him. The day was hot and they were all sweating some. Lawson's eyes were screwed up to keep the sweat and the sun out of them. Through the narrow slits left by his eyelids Delaney was able to discern, though, that he had already made up his mind that his boss's son was guilty as hell.

'Is the Arnold boy badly injured?' Lawson asked.

'Shoulder-wound but he's got a fever,'

Delaney replied.

Lawson didn't need to be told how serious that could be. He could see the pleasure Turner took in the words Delaney had spoken and it told him all he needed to know.

'Wa'al, we can all only pray that he pulls through,' he said, adding, 'ain't that so, Hal?'

Turner showed no sign of acquiescing in what his father's foreman said.

'Ain't that so, Hal?' Lawson repeated more pointedly.

'If you say so, Del,' Turner replied insolently.

Lawson felt like showing him what was what then and there, but instead tipped his hat to Sheriff Delaney and turned his horse around. Delaney watched him and Turner ride away with the others in tow. They kicked up some dust, which blew in his face and it made him turn his own horse around and head back to town. As he spurred it into a trot he somehow felt that this was not by any means the end of the matter. Not by a long shot.

Back in Pecos Red Arnold's fever got worse and Doctor Ritchie began to fear that he might have got blood poisoning. The next twenty-four hours would tell if he was going to live or die.

Early that evening the train from Midland pulled into Pecos station. The Arnolds disembarked from it and made straight for Doctor Ritchie's surgery. The Fourth of July celebrations were not over for everyone and they could hear Bob Wills and his string band playing as they passed Mason's saloon. It filled them both with despair to think of their son lying wounded while the world carried on in its ordinary way. As they passed by the batwing entrance to the saloon Mr Arnold could see everyone dancing and singing along to Will's singularly infectious way of playing dance music and it made his throat tighten and his pace quicken. It made Mrs Arnold's eyes fill with tears. A few minutes later the sight of seeing her son so dangerously ill made those tears all of a sudden flow.

'Tell me exactly what happened, son,' Mr Arnold asked of Jimboy who was sitting at Red's bedside, along with Lucy, when his parents arrived.

At the Five Rings Hal Turner was being similarly quizzed by his father.

'Hal, I just need to know. Did you or did you not shoot Red Arnold?'

Hal at first would not look his father in the eye. He was afraid that he would know he was lying. Then, as his father's questions become more and more pressing, he realized that if he was going to lie it had to be with conviction.

'I told you, Pa,' he said, pulling his shoulders back and holding his head high, 'I did not shoot Red Arnold.'

Turner senior did not believe him but did not say so. He was a man of little patience. If his son chose to lie to him, then so be it.

He had a ranch to run. He didn't have the time to try and tease the truth out of him.

'All right,' he said. 'But there are those who do not believe you. You'd better keep out of their way, which means not going into Pecos for a while. Stay on the ranch and help with the chores.'

'Don't I do that anyway?'

'Hal,' snapped Turner senior, suddenly exasperated, 'you play at it. I'm telling you now to work at it and keep out of the law's way. Do I make myself clear?'

Hal looked at his father insolently. His father had beaten him often enough as a child but he hadn't tried to lift a finger against him since he'd become a man. He felt like daring him to do so now but didn't.

'You're the boss,' he said instead and took his leave.

His insolence left his father indeed wanting to reach for his belt but he knew Hal was too old now to punish in that kind of way. Instead he sent for his foreman and told him to make sure Hal went to the most remote part of the ranch out towards the Trans-Pecos and that he was kept there.

Red's father was no more convinced than Turner senior that Hal had had no part to play in the wounding of his son. He was with Sheriff Delaney demanding that something be done about it.

'I've done all I can for the moment, Dick. We've gotta wait until I can get at the likes of Joey Sands. He knows more than he's letting on but he's too afraid of Hal to let it out,' Sheriff Delaney said.

'This town, Tom! When are you gonna start cleaning it up? I mean, Red's a decent boy, you know that. It just ain't fair that someone like Hal Turner can shoot him down in broad daylight and get away with it,' Arnold senior replied. 'One thing I can assure you, though, is that if Red dies, you can bet your life that Hal will pay for it.'

'Come on now, Dick, talk like that ain't gonna get us anywhere. Up until now you've managed to keep yourself distant from all that goes on in this town.'

'That's because it ain't involved my family before. But now it has. And besides, I might not like Turner nor the way he's built up his ranch, but he ain't part of the scum that washes up in this God-forsaken town. He's a neighbour and his son has near killed mine. At the very least he should be put on trial.'

'He would be if we had any evidence to try him on…'

'Dah!' Arnold spat out in frustration. 'I can see I'm wasting my time here, Tom. Goodbye.'

And with that he stormed out of Sheriff Delaney's office. As he stepped on to the plankwalk he saw through the dark of evening a group of men riding into town down Main Street. Another unruly bunch, he thought to himself, turning and heading in the direction of the doctor's surgery where he'd left his wife. Half an hour later he and his younger son Jimboy rode out of town heading for home, while Mrs Arnold remained in town to help with the nursing of Red. It was still not looking good for Red and the doctor had said he mustn't be moved.

SIX

Sun-up the next day found Dick Arnold standing, with a coffee mug in one hand and a cigarette in the other, on the steps of his ranch house trying to work out what he should do next in the matter of Hal Turner shooting his son. His inclination was to go and beat the truth out of the boy. The town could be rotten but the neighbourhood didn't have to be. It was all that kept going through his mind. Maybe that was what Hal's father had done, beaten it out of him. Maybe he should ride out to the Five Rings and find out. And if his father hadn't... Before he was able to give answer to his thoughts they were interrupted by Jimboy coming out of the house.

'I'm gonna go and see Henry Turner and see what he's gotta say about this.'

What his father told him worried Jimboy. 'You taking me, Pa?' he asked.

'No, I don't think so. Best I go alone.'

'But supposing something happens?'

'That's why it's best you don't come.'

Jimboy wanted to argue but he knew better.

'OK, Pa,' was all he said.

A few minutes passed and then he put a question that had been bothering him to his father.

'Pa, do you think Red'll ever bull-ride again?'

'If he lives,' was all Dick Arnold said in reply. Then he turned and went back into the house to get ready for his ride to the Five Rings.

It was still early July and it was going to be a blisteringly hot day. Dick Arnold was used to that even though he wouldn't normally have taken the chance of riding through near desert terrain in the heat of the day. But he was a desperate man, possessed with anger at what had happened to his son and the law's failure to be able to do anything about it. So he pressed on, riding between orange-tinged mesas, passing deep canyons and shrinking arroyos. For all its forbidding nature it was compellingly beautiful and made him long to have his family whole again. For only then would he again be able to take in pleasure in its gloriously uplifting qualities.

He had ridden well into the day when he saw in the distance what could only have been a small group of men. Turner had not fenced in the west side of his land yet but Arnold knew he was well past its boundaries. The men he could see, he reckoned, must have been cowboys working the ranch. He was riding diagonally to them and knew his path would soon cross theirs. It was not until he was almost upon them that he realized one of them was Hal Turner. As their paths crossed he and the cowboys came to a halt. Hal Turner felt his throat tighten when he saw who the lone rider was. Despite being surrounded by four of his father's men and their foreman, he felt exposed out there in the wilderness.

'Dick,' Del Lawson nodded in greeting to Arnold. 'You're a long way from home.'

'Yeah, well I think you'll know the reason why, Del,' Arnold replied. 'It's riding there right beside you.'

'We're all sorry about Red but Hal here denies he had anything to do with it and there ain't a shred of evidence to implicate him,' Lawson said.

'Let me alone with him for five minutes and I'll get you all the evidence you need.'

Hearing this made Turner all the more edgy. His right hand began to itch, though for the moment he knew it was best to not let it go where it wanted. Instead, he let his tongue have free rein.

'Guess you could say he got what was coming to him. If Lee was still alive he'd have got it long before now.'

'Shut it, Hal,' Lawson turned and snapped at him.

'Why? It's the truth, ain't it? Red stole Lee's gal. Just 'cause he didn't live to do something about it, don't mean to say it should just be forgotten.'

His tone of voice was bitter and vicious and it told Dick Arnold all he needed to know. Spurring his horse, he made it lunge at Turner. As he did so, the cowboys to a man went for their guns.

'All right, all right,' Lawson quickly instructed his men. 'Nobody shoot.'

They all obeyed, except Turner. Arnold was almost upon him and would have taken a bullet at point-blank range had not a rifle-shot slammed into Turner's right shoulder, throwing him from his horse. As Lawson and the cowboys steadied their horses and looked to see where the shot had come from, their guns held high ready to return the fire, Arnold jumped from his horse and pounced on Turner.

'Now, you piece of no-good shit, did you

or did you not shoot my son?' he demanded of him between gritted teeth, taking hold of him with both fists by the front of his shirt.

Before Turner had a chance to reply, Lawson, who'd jumped from his own horse, threw an arm around Arnold's neck and pulled him off. Turner quickly came to his senses and began to look around for his gun, seeing it about a foot away. As he began to reach for it another rifle-shot rang out, sending the gun flying away a few feet. Frightened, Turner rolled on to his back, clutching his shoulder-wound, which was beginning to pain him badly.

'Who's that shooting at us?' Lawson asked Arnold, maintaining his stranglehold on him.

'I don't know, I came alone,' Arnold replied, pulling at Lawson's arm, trying to free himself.

'You sure?' Lawson demanded, tightening his grip.

'I told you so, ain't I?' Arnold replied, choking.

Believing him to be telling the truth, Lawson threw him aside, leaving him to cough and splutter as he tried to catch his breath and ease his strangulated gizzard.

'All right, boys, spread out and go find that son of a bitch, whoever he is,' he ordered the cowboys.

As they rode off, he turned his attentions to Turner. He wasn't hurt too badly, that was for sure. The bullet had only winged him, the flow of blood making the wound look far worse than it really was.

'Get up,' he said to him, 'and let's get you back to the home place and get you patched up.'

Turner put up a good front of being the hard-done-by one. Seeing it made Dick Arnold mad.

'You still haven't answered my question,' he snarled at him, standing up and dusting himself down.

'I think it'd be better if you just dropped the subject for the moment, don't you, Dick?' Lawson said, turning to face him and giving him a telling look. 'I mean, someone just shot Hal and we don't know who did it now, do we?'

'If you're thinking...' Arnold began, but Lawson interrupted him.

'I ain't thinking anything, Dick, at least not until the boys report back, but I'm just saying that perhaps it'd be best if you just got on your horse and rode back home.'

From the look in his eye, Arnold could see that Lawson was trying to give him some friendly advice.

'All right,' he said. Stepping past Lawson to look Turner in the eye, he added, 'But don't think you've heard the last of this. You got off lightly this time, Hal. Someone's gunning for you. I'm not saying I know who, but it's obvious somebody is. They may shoot straighter next time.'

He turned his attention back to Lawson.

'You tell Henry Turner this ain't over yet, not by a long shot. And if my son dies, it ain't never gonna be over.'

Lawson's sympathies lay entirely with

Arnold, but he worked for Henry Turner and it was with him that his loyalties had to lie. He made no reply to Arnold, but simply watched him swing up on to his palomino mount and ride off.

'He's gonna end up the same way Red has, if'n he ain't...' Turner began to say.

But before he could finish the sentence Lawson turned on him and grabbing him by his shirt front, in exactly the same way as Arnold had, said, 'Look here, you little punk, you'd better learn to shut it. I know you shot Red and so does everyone else. You may or may not get away with it this time, but if you don't start learning to respect folks around here, you're gonna come to a sorry end, I can guarantee you that.'

'You're hurting me, Del,' was all Turner said in response, trying to pull himself free from Lawson's grip. The pathetic tone of voice he used angered Lawson and as he freed him he pushed him aggressively away, saying, 'Get mounted.'

The cowboys rode around for some time and Dick Arnold, as he rode home, kept his eye open, but neither of them found who ever it was who'd shot Hal Turner. Jimboy had covered his tracks pretty well. He'd hightailed it out of the area the moment he saw his father ride away from Turner and Lawson. From the moment early that morning when his father had told him he couldn't accompany him to the Five Rings he'd made up his mind to tail his father from a safe distance. The cowboys only worked the area; he'd been born and bred there and knew it like the back of his hand. He easily gave them the slip and was able to get back home ahead enough of his father to put his horse away before he returned.

When he did return, though, his father surprised him with the words, 'That was a damned foolish thing you did back there, son,' adding after a short pause, 'but thanks.'

Jimboy hadn't known that his father had guessed it was him, but now that he knew he had he was proud to think he'd been there when his father needed him. That was a good feeling for a younger son to have. He never said anything in reply to his father as he took the reins from him to take his horse and unsaddle it. It was enough for both of them to know that Hal Turner had at last got some payback for what he'd done to Red.

SEVEN

Three days later Red Arnold was still no better. Doctor Ritchie didn't see that his body could take much more of it. It was only because he was so fit that he had survived this long. He said as much to Sheriff Delaney.

'Well, we can only hope against the odds that he will pull through,' replied the sheriff. 'And what about Hal Turner?'

'That was just a scratch. In a month he won't even remember it happened.'

Sheriff Delaney was not so sure.

'He might want to forget it, but will he be allowed to?'

'Well, I'm glad to say that's your domain and not mine,' Doctor Ritchie replied, getting up from a chair in Delaney's office and taking his leave.

The sheriff remained seated behind his desk. He'd been summoned to the Five Rings and had been told by Turner to find out who had shot his son. Every one guessed it must have been something to do with Dick Arnold but no one had been able to prove anything. Indeed, nobody had wanted to try. Even Turner's attempts at trying to lay the blame on him had been half-hearted. His son had not been seriously wounded and perhaps it would teach him a lesson. He had warned him again to stay away from Pecos. While his shoulder-wound healed he couldn't be forced into any kind of exile in the Trans-Pecos but he could at least be forced to stay at home on the ranch.

Delaney mulled over all of this in his mind while he began to strip and clean one of his two guns. As he did so trouble of a different kind began to brew in Mason's saloon. Members of the gang whom Dick and Jimboy Arnold had a few evenings before seen riding into town were making good with the gals employed to keep men happy by the owners of the saloon. One of them had praised a fellow gang member for being a champion bull-rider and the girl on his lap had remarked that no one could beat Pecos's own champion bull-rider.

'Is that so?' Cody Freeman asked. 'Well, where is this man? I gotta meet him?'

'Well, he ain't in much of a fit state to meet anyone at the moment,' another of the good-time gals remarked. 'He's lying half-dead in the doctor's treatment rooms.'

Cody Freeman, who'd been more or less drunk since he rode into town with the others, suddenly looked very concerned.

'He get throwed or gored?' he asked.

'Shot,' replied Suzie, the girl on his lap.

Freeman studied her for a while and then said, 'Well, that sure is an unfitting way for a bull-rider to go.'

'He ain't gone nowhere yet but folks say it can't be long. Mind you, some would say he got what was coming to him.'

Freeman questioned Suzie about what she meant and she explained the whole sorry story to him. By the end of it he was indignant enough on behalf of a man whom he took to be a comrade, even if he'd never met him, that he was ready to go look for Hal Turner and make him pay for what he'd done to Red Arnold.

'Nobody harms a bull-rider and gets away with it,' he said. 'Do they, Pete?' he called out to one of his sidekicks, who was similarly drunk and preoccupied with a good-time gal.

'No, no,' Pete Hammer replied once he was made to understand what Freeman was on about.

Then the word went all round the gang

until at last all of them were itching to make good use of an excuse that had suddenly come their way to make trouble. Cody Freeman wasn't really a champion bull-rider. He had once ridden bulls when he'd worked on a ranch and had been a natural at it but that had all ended when he got fired for being headstrong and unwilling to take orders. All of the members of the gang he was with now were similarly unemployable and lived from cattle-rustling. But when full of drink and wanting to impress a lady Cody Freeman romanticized himself into being something more than a cow thief and his friends were happy enough to indulge him.

'So, where would we find the yellow-belly who shot this champion bull-rider?' he asked.

Joey – Hal Turner's number one admirer – happened to be close by and overheard the conversation that had gone on between Suzie and Cody Freeman. He was with other members of the gang who had grouped around Hal Turner and they all looked from one to the other as the conversation developed. They all reckoned themselves tough but knew Cody Freeman and his friends to be tougher still. All of them, that is, except Joey, who lived only to prove to his hero Turner that he was worthy of his friendship.

'Why?' he jumped up and asked in answer to Freeman's question. 'What you gonna do about it?'

Freeman turned and glared at him. When he saw what he thought of as a little runt trying to look something he wasn't he sat back, saying, 'I'm gonna kill him.'

As he said it he burst out laughing and so did his friends with him. It made Joey feel stupid, which, though it was a feeling he was well used to, was one he resented bitterly.

'You wouldn't be saying that if he was here,' he said, which served only to make Cody Freeman and his friends laugh more loudly.

Then suddenly Freeman stopped laughing. Pushing Suzie from his lap, he got up and turned to face Joey. He felt tempted to plug him full of lead but, unusually for him, took pity on him.

'Now what makes you think that?' he asked.

Joey looked uneasy to be facing the man eyeball to eyeball and it showed in the nervous way he held himself. Though he was not with Hal Turner he was with others of the gang and did not want to lose face.

''Cause I know him,' he replied.

'You do? Then tell me what makes him shoot a man when he's riding a bull and can't shoot back or get out of the way even?'

Joey was about to tell him when one of the other members of the gang jumped in with, 'Who says he did?'

'That's right,' Joey quickly said, suddenly looking flustered.

Cody Freeman simply roared with laughter at what he realized had nearly happened.

'Oh, I see,' he said throwing a quick look at his friends. 'Well, tell your friend...' he began, then asked, 'What's your name, son?'

Joey told him.

'Joey? OK, Joey, tell your friend I'm looking for him.'

Joey knew he was in way over his head and decided it was time for him to get out.

'I will,' he said.

Cody Freeman eyeballed the kid for a few seconds longer and then turned his attention back to Suzie. As he sat down and put her back on his knee, Joey breathed a deep sigh of relief. But he couldn't wait to go and find Hal Turner and tell him what had happened. He beat a tactical retreat and the others went with him.

'Why'd you poke your nose in at all, Joey? Look at the trouble you nearly got me into before, opening your big mouth.'

Joey had found Hal Turner sitting on the veranda at the ranch house at the Five Rings. He'd arrived alone and Hal had walked him away from the house, so as to avoid other folk, meaning in particular his father, overhearing anything controversial

Joey might have to say.

'I know, Hal, but I didn't like hearing them saying the things they was saying about you. I mean, he said you was yella for firing at Red when he was unarmed and not looking.'

Hal turned and looked at Joey for a moment without saying anything. He thought of his brother and found himself feeling mean towards Red Arnold all over again. He always did when he thought of the brother he had so idolized and of how he had died, reckoning that if he hadn't have been so upset over Red stealing his girl-friend he wouldn't have let the bull get the better of him. He'd have been here now – and would have whipped Red at this year's and every year's rodeo.

'OK,' he said to Joey. 'Maybe I ought to go into town and shut that shit's mouth up.'

As he said it he jarred his shoulder and the pain of doing so made him wince.

'What about your shoulder?' Joey asked.

'I can still shoot,' was all Hal said in reply,

but he looked over his good shoulder to make sure his father wasn't anywhere close by and listening. He was convinced that Dick Arnold had something to do with his being shot at; maybe his father was content to do nothing about it, but that didn't mean to say he had to be.

EIGHT

As Hal Turner sneaked away from the Five Rings, Dick Arnold was hearing the good news, that Red had turned the corner.

'Yeah,' said Doctor Ritchie, 'his fever's gone and his temperature is about normal.'

'That's wonderful, Doctor!' exclaimed Arnold. He had just stepped into Doctor Ritchie's surgery. 'Can I see him?'

Doctor Ritchie showed him into the room where Red had been 'hospitalized' and where he was still being tended to by his mother and Lucy. He hurried to his son's bedside and standing affectionately over him, asked, 'How are you, son? Doctor says you're on the mend.'

As he spoke he looked at his wife and smiled. She came and stood beside him and he put an arm around her.

'I'm OK, Pa. How's Jimboy and the ranch?' Red replied, weakly, looking from his father to Lucy, whose heart melted with the all-consuming tenderness, which, having nearly lost him, she now felt for him.

'They're both fine, son. Both fine. But don't you worry about them. You just concentrate on getting better,' Arnold replied.

Red had asked both his mother and Lucy if they'd found out who shot him but they had evaded the question. Red, though, wanted to know. Or rather he wanted to know if what he suspected was true.

'Who shot me, Pa?' he asked in what everyone knew to be his direct manner.

'We still don't know, son, at least not for sure. Sheriff Delaney is still working on it.'

The anger Dick Arnold had felt on first seeing his son lying so ill surfaced again now as he thought about what little in fact was being done to bring Hal Turner to book. Red read it in his face.

'It was Hal, weren't it?' he said.

Dick Arnold was about to answer him, when his wife interrupted, saying, 'You can worry about that later, son. For the moment you've got to concentrate on getting better.'

'I know, Ma, but I just gotta know,' Red said insistently.

'He's got a right to know, Sal,' Dick Arnold remarked.

'All right, Dick,' Sal Arnold agreed, 'but then he must rest.'

'Was it, Pa?' Red asked.

Lucy took his hand in hers and her eyes filled.

'Everybody reckons so but there ain't no proof,' Dick Arnold replied. He omitted to tell him of what had happened on the edge of the Trans-Pecos when Hal himself had been shot.

Red looked pensive for a moment and then said, 'Does that mean he's gonna get away with it?'

Before Dick Arnold could answer Doctor Ritchie came into the room and said that he thought Red should be left now to rest in case overtiring him brought back the fever. Sally Arnold agreed with him.

'Yes, come on now, Dick, Red must rest if he's to get better. And surely you've got work to do on the ranch,' she said, beginning to busy herself about her son's sickbed.

She knew that in the West if someone committed a wrong they had to pay for it and she didn't like thinking that her son's differences with Hal Turner might not be over yet.

'Doctor Ritchie and your mama are right, son. You just concentrate on getting well,' Dick Arnold said to Red. 'And maybe then we can set about planning the biggest wedding there's ever been in these parts,' he added, looking at Lucy and giving her an appreciatively indulgent smile. Blushing, she averted her gaze.

'Yes, yes, Dick Arnold,' his wife replied, shooing him out of the room. 'There's time enough yet to be thinking of things like that.'

Dick Arnold next called on Sheriff Delaney, whom he found in his office looking through a number of Wanted notices that had just arrived.

'Good morning to you, Dick,' Sheriff Delaney greeted him as he came through the door. 'How's our wounded soldier today?'

Arnold nodded a greeting and then replied, 'A lot better, Tom, thanks. The fever has broken and he's talking sense again, thank God.'

'Well, that's very good news,' Delaney remarked.

Something, though, told him it wasn't entirely good news.

'Coffee?' he asked of Arnold.

'Don't mind if I do,' replied Arnold.

As Delaney got up from his desk to go and pour him a coffee from a pot on a stove Arnold caught sight of the Wanted notices he'd been reading.

'That's quite a bundle you've got there,' he remarked.

'Yeah,' replied Delaney, 'seems the West just gets wilder.'

'And Pecos wilder with it.'

Tension suddenly filled the air and Delaney felt he knew what was coming next. And he was right.

'Tom, what's to be done about the Turner boy?'

Delaney finished pouring the coffee before he replied.

'Well,' he began, handing Dick Arnold a tin mug of coffee, 'there still ain't no proof he did it and nor is there likely to be any. That's the long and short of it, Dick, and it leaves my hands tied.'

Arnold thought for a moment. The picture of his eldest son lying near death's door filled his head and he couldn't get it out. 'Not mine, though,' he found himself saying.

'Dick, I don't need to tell you who's the law in Pecos. I know who it was who had a crack at Turner. If he'd died from that shot you'd have been held as an accomplice.'

'But you can't say who fired that shot at Hal any more than you know who fired at Red,' Arnold stated.

'Yeah, well ... I got my own views on that,' Delaney said. 'You was lucky, that's all I gotta say on it.'

Arnold made no reply and Delaney carried on, 'Red got shot, Hal got shot. Don't you think that just about makes things even?'

Arnold did not think so and it showed in his face. Winging and near murder were poles apart, he couldn't help but think to himself.

'Well, Tom,' he replied, 'and I don't mean any disrespect in this, but it's often been said the law's an ass.'

Delaney did not get a chance to reply to what Arnold had said, for suddenly his deputy came into his office. After greeting Arnold the deputy said to him,

'Those boys getting rowdy again, Tom. There's talk of them setting up some bull-riding in the courthouse square.'

'Is there? Well, we'll see about that,' Delaney replied, getting up from his desk and reaching for his gun and holster, which were hanging on the wall behind him. The deputy's arrival brought this and Arnold's meeting to a close and both men bid one another goodbye, with Delaney reminding Arnold of what he'd said. Arnold made no reply, his mind again full of the picture of Red lying in bed with a high fever and talking gibberish. It made him angry and think again that the law was an ass.

Cody Freeman and Peter Hammer were indeed trying to organize a bull-riding competition. They were in Mason's saloon. Freeman was standing up at the bar challenging other drinkers to a bull-ride.

'And where we gonna ride these bulls?' a cowboy called out. 'The rodeo's over. You're about ten days too late.'

'You don't need no rodeo to ride bulls,' Hammer replied in answer.

All those involved in the discussion were drunk and swaying and slurring their words.

'That's true, I suppose,' another cowboy said.

'All right,' said Cody. 'All we gotta do then is find us a few bulls. Now who's up for it?'

It was at this point that Sheriff Delaney's deputy, who had happened to drop into the saloon and overhear what was being planned, had gone to get the sheriff. By the time he arrived back at the saloon with Delaney, Freeman and Hammer had as good as got their bull-riding competition organized. Cody Freeman hated the law and was never happier than when he was baiting lawmen.

'Oh!' he exclaimed out loud on seeing Delaney and his deputy come through the batwings of Mason's. 'Look who's come to join in the party.' Keeping his eyes on the two men, he asked Delaney, 'You any good at bull-riding, Sheriff?'

'There ain't gonna be any bull-riding,' was Delaney's reply. 'At least not in Pecos. The rodeo's over for this year.'

'That's just what I said,' remarked the cowboy who'd made the point earlier.

'Well, does there have to be a rodeo to have a bull-riding?' Freeman asked, gesticulating with a hand he was holding a beer-glass in and adopting a sassy pose.

'In my town there does,' was Sheriff Delaney's reply.

'Your town?' Freeman asked derisively, casting an eye about the saloon. 'Don't Pecos belong to its citizens?'

Cowboys who'd hung around Pecos for long enough to feel it was their home, let Delaney know they agreed with him.

'See,' Freeman said, turning back to face the sheriff. 'And you all want a bull-riding, don't you?' he asked of the gathering.

'Yeah,' they all answered with one voice.

Looking him squarely in the eye Freeman tried to face Sheriff Delaney down.

'You can have your bull-riding, anywhere you want,' Delaney told him, 'but in Pecos.'

The look Freeman saw in Delaney's eyes told him he meant business. He might have gone for his gun in an attempt to settle the matter had not the batwing doors of the saloon suddenly been forced apart to let Joey and Hal Turner gain entrance. Freeman did not at first recognize Joey and the appearance of a couple of anonymous-looking cowboys entering the saloon meant nothing to him. But the appearance of Turner meant a great deal to the sheriff.

As he came through the batwings Turner could see there was some kind of a situation going on but instead of it causing him to pause he strode on past Delaney to the bar. Joey followed and as he came closer to the bar he was recognized by Freeman. Sheriff Delaney had decided that he should take Turner aside and warn him to keep out of

91

Dick Arnold's way, but before he got a chance to do so Freeman suddenly said,

'Hey, ain't you the dude that was boasting your sidekick had shot this hole of a town's champion bull-rider?'

Joey looked first at Freeman and then quickly at Delaney. 'I ain't never said such a thing to nobody,' he replied.

'You sure did, didn't he, boys?' Freeman insisted.

Peter Hammer and the others backed him up. Turner felt as if he could have killed Joey, who was suddenly looking panicky.

'I don't know what he's talking about,' Joey blurted out to Sheriff Delaney.

Hal Turner kept his cool, waiting to see how Delaney was going to react.

'All right, now both of you shut it!' Delaney snarled. 'I've heard that one and it's been investigated.'

'Well, who cares who shot who? It ain't no business of ours. What we want is a bull-riding,' Freeman remarked.

'And I told you,' Delaney said, 'there ain't

gonna be one in Pecos.'

'Ah, shucks, Sheriff, why not?' Turner spoke up. 'I mean, it's a long time 'til the next Fourth of July and the last one weren't never finished anyway. No one got the prize for being champion rider.'

'You want to finish off last Fourth of July's rodeo best you go see the mayor about it, but in the meantime there ain't gonna be no bull-riding in Pecos. Do I make myself clear?'

The idea of continuing the Fourth of July rodeo seemed to satisfy everyone and the heat quickly went out of the situation. The place began again to fill with the hum of conversation and Sheriff Delaney decided he could make an exit. But not before talking to Turner. He looked over at him and as he did so Turner's eyes turned to meet his. They were full of anticipation of the telling-off every delinquent expects when he comes up against real authority.

'Red Arnold's father is in town. I suggest you keep out of his way,' Delaney said, walking up to him.

'If he keeps out of mine,' Turner replied insolently.

'Or, you can spend your time in Pecos in the cells. Is that understood?'

Turner did not make a reply, but turned away from Delaney and picked up a beer the barkeep had put down on the counter. Delaney was the kind of law-enforcer who knew that delinquent youth was generally its own worst enemy, most of its insolence being mere bravado. It rarely turned to pure criminality as youth grew up and he reckoned the best way of dealing with Turner was to ignore his bad behaviour until the rope he was given turned into the noose that would hang him. Casting his eye about the gathering and deciding he'd nipped in the bud any trouble that might have been brewing, he left, with his deputy hot on his heels.

NINE

Red Arnold's fever had gone and he was beginning to show signs of making a good recovery. Doctor Ritchie had said it would be safe for him to move in a few days' time. This pleased everyone. His mother simply wanted to go home, he wanted to get up and Sheriff Delaney wanted the Arnolds and Hal Turner to be as far apart as possible until the matter between them had been resolved. While preparations were being made for Red to go home the mayor of Pecos was considering the request Cody Freeman and Hal Turner had put to him for a bull-riding to be staged to complete the unfinished events of the rodeo.

'Well, I don't know, Hal,' Mayor Duncan was saying to Hal Turner. The Turner family, being big ranchers, were influential people in and around Pecos and normally the mayor would oblige them if he could. But in this instance Sheriff Delaney had been having his say. 'The rodeo's over and folks have been saying that the un-won bull-riding championship should go to Red, with what happened and all. In fact, it's all but been decided by the rodeo committee.'

'Well, dang it, that ain't right,' Hal Turner insisted.

He didn't have an argument as to why it shouldn't be right and just carried on like a spoilt brat wanting to get his own way.

'I'd like to oblige you, son,' Mayor Duncan remarked, remembering who his father was.

'Well, to hell with the rodeo,' Freeman declared. 'Can't we just have a bull-riding? I mean is we in cowboy country or ain't we?'

'I told you, cowboy,' Delaney stated firmly, 'Red Arnold was gunned down while mounted on a bull's back and people in this town ain't happy about it. You go mounting another bull-riding in this town and you're likely to upset them even more. And besides, apart from you, who else is gonna take part in it?'

Without hesitating Freeman replied, 'Why, Hal here. It's only gonna be a competition between him and me.'

'Me?' Turner exclaimed. 'I ain't no bull-rider.'

'Sure you are,' Freeman declared. 'I've heard all sorts of stories from your pal about how good you Turner boys are at staying on a bull.'

'My brother, maybe, but he's dead and I ain't never took to it.'

A look of meanness suddenly spread across Freeman's face. 'I said, boy, you is gonna ride against me and that is what you're gonna do.'

'But my arm...' Turner began.

'You only need one hand to hold on,' Freeman replied. Then turning to Mayor Duncan, he asked, 'Now can we have this bull-riding or not?'

The mayor looked at Sheriff Delaney and indicated with the expression on his face that it was up to him. Delaney decided that the way out of what could grow into a feud between the Arnolds and the Turners was for the town to see Hal Turner made a complete fool of. 'OK,' he said. 'But you gotta let the Arnolds compete alongside you. The championship would have been Red's but for what happened. It might make the town happy if it goes to someone else in his family.'

'Suits me fine,' Freeman replied.

Turner realized he had no choice but to go along with it. Besides, he thought to himself, Jimboy Arnold was no more a bull-rider than he was and he couldn't see his father competing, not at his age.

'Hal?' the mayor asked.

'Sure he agrees to it, don't you, boy?' Freeman replied for him, throwing an arm around him and making his shoulder-wound hurt.

Wincing and pulling away, Turner indicated no particular objection. And the bull-riding was arranged for the following

Saturday, which was only two days away. It wasn't long before the whole town and its environs got to hear of it.

'You're gonna what?' Dick Arnold exclaimed when told by Jimboy that he was going to enter.

Jimboy had gone into town the day the bull-riding was arranged to visit his brother in Doctor Ritchie's surgery. His father had ridden home earlier.

'I said there's a bull-riding been arranged in town for Saturday and I'm competing in it.'

'There weren't no talk of bull-riding in town when I was there this morning.'

'Yeah, well it's all been arranged. Hal Turner's riding in it and Sheriff Delaney said he thought I should.'

'But you ain't no bull-rider, son.'

'No more's Hal Turner, but I can whip him, it'll make up some for his shooting Red,' Jimboy enthused.

Dick Arnold was not convinced and it showed in his face. It was near sundown and he was sitting on his veranda, smoking.

'I gotta day to practise in, Pa, and I seen Red do it often enough to know how it should be done.'

'Knowing and doing ain't the same thing, son,' Arnold senior replied, his expression pensive and his brow furrowed. He was thinking that if Jimboy could outride Hal it would surely be something.

'I gotta do it, Pa. I just gotta.'

'And if Hal Turner should win?' Dick Arnold asked.

'He won't. Not if I ride, Pa. He won't.'

Arnold thought for a moment. He'd never seen his son so serious about anything. 'All right,' he said. 'All right.'

They'd practise on the bull Red kept himself fit on. It weighed about 2,000 pounds and was easily riled. It was tall with long, lean legs and because he danced about like a dog when ridden Red had called him Wolfman. It was just after sun-up when they started.

'Lucky your ma ain't here, son. Otherwise

I don't think we'd be doing this.'

Jimboy was too nervous to reply. As he stood looking at Wolfman in his pen his heart was pounding and his stomach turning. In his hand he held the rope that he was somehow or other going to have to pluck up the nerve to tie around Wolfman's belly to give him something to hold on to. Luckily, Wolfman had proved the kind of bull that was quiet until a man got on his back. But then he went wild, bucking and twisting until he threw him off. Jimboy had watched his brother walk slowly up to him and in a dazzling second throw the rope over him, grab it from underneath and tie it tight. It looked easy but he knew it wasn't.

'OK, son,' his father advised him. 'Just remember, watch his shoulders and keep your hand held high. With the other hold on and sit tight, with your heels pushed down.'

Jimboy was thrown a dozen times before he got the hang of it. He didn't take to it as naturally as Red but as the day wore on he managed to remain on the bull's back a respectable length of time and when he was thrown he broke no bones. Later that day when he and his father were eating supper, his father said to him, 'You told Red and your ma about this?'

'No, but they probably heard about it by now. The town was fairly humming with it by time I left to ride home. They was bound to hear about it before long.'

Both father and son knew exactly what Red and Sally would have to say on the matter.

'They'll take some persuading to see any sense in what you're gonna do, son,' Dick Arnold remarked.

Jimboy made no reply. His thoughts were beginning to be far away. In them was a picture of Hal Turner hunkering down on the roof of the courthouse and taking aim with a rifle. Then it turned to a picture of Red being thrown from the bull, not by its bucking, but by the force of the bullet smashing into his shoulder. Whatever his brother or mother said, he knew he had to go through with the bull-riding tomorrow and beat Hal Turner. He could have wished that the shot he fired at Hal Turner out on the Trans-Pecos had killed him but he knew that if he could beat him at bull-riding it would be a humiliation hard to play down.

'I don't like there being so many guns in town,' Sheriff Delaney remarked to his deputy.

'It was bound to happen, Tom. Word gets out pretty quickly in these parts and a bull-riding ain't something folks is gonna want to miss.'

'Yeah, well, that may be. But there's a lot of tension in town being fuelled by a lot of liquor. Whoever wins the bull-riding, it's gonna leave one side feeling mighty mean.'

'I don't think we have to worry too much about the Arnolds.'

'Maybe not, but Cody Freeman seems somehow or other to be on their side. I don't quite understand it myself.'

'It gives him a cause, I suppose. Most young men like a fraternity to feel part of.

His is bull-riders. The rumour is Turner shot Red, a fellow bull-rider, and Cody feels it's his duty to do some avengin'.'

'Yeah, well not in my town.'

By lunch time a makeshift arena was almost complete and buckboards and bulls were arriving. Red Arnold had got to hear what was happening and he was cursing his wounded shoulder.

'It should be me out there getting ready to ride, not Jimboy. He ain't no bull-rider,' he said to Lucy.

'Hal Turner isn't any more of one. And your father said Jimboy did pretty good yesterday. Better than he'd have thought,' Lucy remarked in her usually soothing tones.

Sally Arnold was not there. She'd gone to remonstrate with her husband and Jimboy in the hope of getting them to withdraw from what she saw as a damn fool exercise.

'If Hal shot me, and I guess everyone knows it was him, then the quarrel with him is mine, not Jimboy's.'

'It's the whole town's, Red. I don't understand the way you men carry on but I do know my father and brothers would not be happy to let anyone get away with shooting one of us.'

Red thought for a moment, frustration and anger written all over his face. The wound in his shoulder had not completely stopped festering and he was still weak.

'Damn this shoulder!' he suddenly exclaimed.

'Red, Red, don't,' Lucy said in calming tones. 'That's not going to help.'

'I thought Pa said Hal had been shot. How come he's up to getting on a bull?'

'It was just a flesh wound. Maybe it'll give Jimboy the advantage. But you haven't got to worry about that, Red. You've just got to concentrate on getting better.'

'Yeah, yeah,' was all Red said in reply, his voice full of angry impatience with life.

The bull-riding was set for 2.30 in the

afternoon. It was gone noon, the sun was high in the sky and it was going to be a hot, blistering afternoon. There'd already been one shoot-out in one of the town's saloons. It was nothing to do with Cody Freeman and his gang, nor the trouble between Hal Turner and the Arnolds, but it was a sign that the afternoon's bull-riding was not the family affair the Fourth of July rodeo normally was.

TEN

'Why couldn't I have drawn Wolfman?'

'Jimboy, son, most of life's a lottery. It's what we do with the chances it throws up at us that makes the difference. You can ride, I seen that for myself. Maybe you ain't had enough practice yet, but you can do it. What bull you're on ain't gonna make a lot of difference.'

His father's reasoning didn't convince Jimboy. He'd never had an inclination to go bull-riding and didn't have one now. He was doing it only because he wasn't going to let Hal Turner walk away with any sort of crown for bull-riding in Pecos. The crown belonged to Red and if Red wasn't in a position to compete for it himself, then he had to do it for him. Bull-riding was still in a primitive stage in the early 1890s. It couldn't yet be called a sport, but was simply a show-off affair that had its origins in derring-do: 'Bucking bronc! I bet you I can stay on a steer's back longer than any man here!' And so a new game was born to show just how wildly courageous a cowboy out West could really be.

'Your pa's right.'

It was Mickey, who, along with a number of others, had come along to support the Arnolds.

'You ride him then,' Jimboy muttered to himself, as he pulled on a pair of Red's old chaps.

'Right, then,' Dick Arnold, realising the offer was not going to be taken up, said, 'let's get over there.'

They walked the fifty or so feet from the place where they'd parked their buckboards to the arena. There was quite a crowd of cowboys, ranchers and townsfolk. They were all male, the occasion not being deemed a family affair. An occasional gunshot was heard being fired into the air by riotous cowboys cavorting about on horseback. Some of the younger bucks even raced one another down the length of Main Street, making their horses rear up, and pretending they were riding in a rodeo. Sheriff Delaney and his deputies recognized such activity as youthful exuberance and turned a blind eye to it for the moment. It was harmless enough and the participants would soon dash off to watch the bull-riding once it got started.

Turner showed up with Joey and his pals. His father had no interest in coming to town with him, though he knew what was happening. In his place he sent his foreman, Del Lawson. Lawson had no liking for Hal and hadn't wanted to get involved but did what his boss told him to do. In Pecos, he left Hal and his pals to their own devices and went to Mason's saloon, where he proposed to spend the day drinking and having fun with a couple of his favourite good-time gals.

It was the usual practice for the participants in a rodeo event to bring their own animals, which were put in a pool. Which animal they'd ride was decided by drawing lots. Hal Turner drew the Arnolds' bull, Wolfman. Jimboy Arnold drew his, a mean looking brahma which weighed more than 2,000 pounds and looked as if it hated all humans. Cody Freeman drew a less fiery looking bull but one which seemed to kick out its legs at anything that passed out of sheer habit.

Arenas didn't have shoots in those early days, the bulls were simply tied to the back of buckboards and kept at bay until needed. That in itself produced a fair amount of excitement, with bulls occasionally getting away and running amok through the spectators. But this was all part of the excitement of the day. Today's excitement though was fuelled not by the excitement of sport, but by the tension of the antagonism that existed between the Arnolds and Hal Turner. The talk was all of how folks knew Hal Turner had shot Red Arnold and of how they all hoped Jimboy paid him back in plenty. Cody Freeman was an unknown quantity, a low-life blow-in, who simply made up the numbers, even if the event had been his idea in the first place.

As the event got under way, it fell to Cody Freeman to be the first to ride. There was no eight-second bell in those days. You simply stayed on until you were thrown off.

'You ready to get on?' his sidekick Pete Hammer asked him.

'Ready as I'll ever be,' Freeman replied, spitting out a mouthful of chawing-tobacco juice.

As Hammer and two other men kept a

long-horn, whose horns were so long it was called Hightower, quiet, Freeman mounted him. As he did so he threw a rope around the beast's waist. Keeping well clear of Hightower's horns, Hammer grabbed the rope and handed it back to Freeman, who pulled it tight and held it fast in the hand he'd use to hold on once the ride started. Getting his seat right and feeling that his grip was as sure as it was going to be he spat out the words that told Hammer and his aids to let Hightower go. They did so, on the instant turning and leaping to safety over the arena fence.

Hightower began to spin almost immediately, firstly, in a 360-degree circle to the left and then instantly in one to the right. As he did so, Freeman felt a centrifugal force pulling him down hard on to the bull's back. Seeing this had not unseated him, Hightower began to buck, kicking his hind legs high into the air, forcing Freeman, if he was to avoid being skewered on the bull's lethal-looking horns, to throw back his torso and straighten his legs, forcing his heels down and pulling his toes back. The crowd of spectators cheered him on.

Hammer's mouth simply hung open. He'd seen Freeman ride and knew he was good but never this good. Ten and fifteen seconds passed and still he remained seated. Then Hightower bucked so wildly it looked as if he'd break his back. Freeman's iron grip began to weaken and he felt himself being thrown forwards. His objective then was to avoid Hightower's horns. Not holding much hope of doing so, he was saved by Hightower's suddenly going into a spin. Instead of crashing on to the horns, Freeman found himself being thrown to the right and almost beating his head against the bull's meaty thighs. Hightower next leapt high into the air and as he came down Freeman felt himself continuing to go up. In the next instance Hightower was gone from under him and he fell in a heap to the ground. As the crowd roared and cheered, and some fired into the air, Hammer and his aids leapt into the arena. While his aids distracted the bull to stop it from trying to gore Freeman, Hammer helped him up.

'You all right, pardner?' he asked. 'That's gonna take some beating,' he added as he hurried Freeman limping and catching his breath out of the arena. Both Hal Turner and Jimboy Arnold had watched in awe as Freeman completed his remarkable ride. Neither thought they stood a chance in hell of bettering it and both were mighty grateful their bulls were not longhorns.

It was Hal Turner's turn next.

'You won't beat that, Hal,' Joey said to him, 'but all you gotta do is stay on long enough to beat Jimboy.'

His shoulder-wound was healing nicely but it still hurt if jarred and it had been jarred a lot in the last twenty-four hours as he practised trying to get on a bull and just stay on. As he ran a hand over it, he felt like punching Joey. If Joey hadn't been drinking in the saloon that day and shooting his mouth off, he wouldn't be in the predicament he was in now. He'd never felt inclined to get up on a bull's back and ride it and he didn't want to now.

'Shut up, Joey,' he snapped.

Joe was hurt by his hero's sharpness but he knew better than to show it. He knew he'd got him into something that could end in humiliation for him and he wished there was something he could do about it. But what was there? The few grey brain-cells he had began in earnest to try and come up with something.

'Hold it, then!' Turner snarled at his aids, as Wolfman tried to break free from their hold.

'You ready to do it?' one of them asked.

'Ready as I'll ever be,' replied Turner.

'Right, throw us one end of the rope.'

Turner did so. Then he put a glove on his right hand, pulling it tight to make sure his fingers went in as far as they could. Then he flexed them.

'Right. Get on.'

He climbed up on to the arena fence and

without hesitating got from it on to Wolf-man's back. The bull wriggled a bit but did not seem to object particularly to the burden now on his back, but that was until Turner's aids let it go.

'Right, you ready, Hal?'

'Yeah, go!' Turner replied, his mouth barely wet enough to let his tongue work.

Wolfman took off. Turner was using his left hand to hold on. He'd hardly lifted his right arm to hold it above his head, when he found himself suddenly being thrown to the left. His legs went up behind him and spun him 360 degrees. Only trouble was, his left hand was still in place, gripping the rope. As Joey, his aids and the crowd looked on in horror, Wolfman twisted, first to the left and then to the right, trying to shake him off. This was humiliation indeed. Turner thought his arm was going to break, as he found himself being bounced and dragged along. At last the rope loosened and he was able to pull his hand free. He hit the dust hard on his right side, tearing open his shoulder-wound and leaving him in agony. His left arm had not been broken, but as he tried to bring it to his left shoulder it hurt like hell. Soon his aids were with him, helping him to his feet and all but carrying him out of the arena. Joey, like the rest of the crowd, looked on in silence. He'd had an idea of what he could do to make things up to Turner, but had shied away from it. Now, after seeing him so humiliated, he reckoned he had to do it.

As Joey began to slip away through the crowd in the direction of the courthouse, voices could be heard remarking on the fact that Hal Turner was not the rider his elder brother had been. Adding that, on the strength of today's performance, he never would be.

Red Arnold knew what had happened within minutes of Hal Turner biting the dust.

'Good old Wolfman!' he exclaimed glee-fully from his sick-bed to the boy, Mickey's younger brother, who'd brought him the news.

Looking on, Lucy and his mother did not share his joy.

'It means things do not bode well for Jimboy,' Sally Arnold declared. 'He is no more practised at bull-riding, an altogether lunatic pastime, if you ask me, than is Hal Turner.'

'Oh, Red, shouldn't we try and stop him?' Lucy asked in concerned tones.

'Red can do nothing from his sick-bed,' his mother reminded Lucy in matronly tones.

'We cannot stop him,' Red said. 'Especially not now. It would look like cowardice.'

But even as he said it Red was fearful for his younger brother's safety.

'Damn this shoulder of mine,' he complained bitterly, not for the first time. 'It should be me out there riding, not Jimboy.'

'That may be so,' his mother reassured him, 'but it can't be helped.'

'But if anything should happen to Jimboy...'

'Your father is with him. He'll make sure nothing does, surely,' Lucy interrupted him.

Before Red could answer a loud cheer set up by the crowd of spectators watching the bull-riding was carried on the wind to Doctor Ritchie's surgery.

'Sounds like it's too late to do anything now,' Mickey's brother declared, rushing out of the room.

He was right, for Jimboy was already launched on his ride on the Turners' bull, a Hereford called Blacker Than Hell. And the crowd was cheering him because he was keeping his seat. He might not have the inclination that his brother had to ride bulls but he was demonstrating that he was not lacking in his brother's natural given talent for it. Blacker Than Hell was spinning like a Dervish but, holding his free hand high, Jimboy was going with it. Then when he bucked, keeping his eyes steadfastly fixed, as any professional would, and as his father told him he must, firm on the beast's shoulders, he remained firmly in place. Ten seconds or more had passed and the crowd was going mad. Jimboy was going to last

118

longer than Cody Freeman.

But it was something Joey, who was up on the courthouse roof, could not bear to let happen. Hunkered down on the very spot his hero had taken aim from when he shot Red Arnold, he was trying to keep Jimboy in the sights of a Winchester .44 rifle. But it was not easy. He didn't want to kill Jimboy, just knock him from the bull. His nerves, though, were getting the better of him and sweat was rolling down his face and getting in his eyes, making it hard for him to see. And the seconds were ticking by. In the end he just pulled the trigger. Blacker Than Hell had just kicked his hind-legs high into the air when the bullet slapped into the wall of his chest and tore straight into his heart. His front legs buckled and on the instant he fell to the ground, leaving Jimboy with barely enough time to jump clear. No one heard the shot but they saw the blood as it began to pour from the bull's wound and they all knew what had happened – for a second time.

For Dick Arnold it all happened in slow motion. But real time found him leaping over the arena fence and rushing to his son's side.

'Someone shot him from under me, Pa,' Jimboy blurted out as his father's hands reached out to help him up.

Taking in the sight of Blacker Than Hell's blood soaking into the dirt, Dick Arnold cast his gaze above the heads of the crowd. It fell upon the courthouse roof. His eyesight was better than average and what he saw on the roof of the courthouse made his blood boil. There was someone up there. Making a getaway for sure, but not fast enough.

'Take care of Jimboy,' he said to Mickey, who'd reached Jimboy's side seconds after he had.

'Sure thing, Mr Arnold, but...'

Mickey got no further. Dick Arnold was already running in the direction of the courthouse. Cody Freeman and Pete Hammer, both of whose eyes had not left the arena since Blacker Than Hell had fallen, guessed he'd seen something and began to push their way through the crowd after him. The members of their gang who'd acted as Freeman's aids followed them.

'Where they going?' Hal Turner asked.

He'd looked on dumbfounded as one of his father's prize bulls became destined for the butcher's, knowing there'd be hell to pay when he got home.

'Search me,' one of his gang replied.

'Hang on a minute,' said Turner, looking around him. 'Where's Joey?'

As one they all looked in the direction of the courthouse roof.

'That dang fool!' Turner muttered to himself, as he began to get his bruised and sore body back into fighting mode.

ELEVEN

Sheriff Delaney soon got to know that something untoward had happened. From the start of the day's proceedings the air had been full of the sound of gunfire. But somehow it had lost its festive tone and become angry. Something told him he'd better go and investigate. As he stepped out on to the boardwalk outside his office he was greeted by the worried-looking face of one of his deputies.

'What is it?' he said to him.

'There's been another shooting, Sheriff.'

'What d'you mean, another shooting?' Delaney asked him.

'Someone shot the bull from under Jim-boy Arnold as he was riding in the arena.'

'Not again,' Delaney remarked, stepping off the boardwalk and heading in the direction of the arena. 'Is he hurt?'

'No, he ain't, but there's gonna be trouble.'

'Where was Turner?'

'Standing by the arena. It weren't him this time.'

'Hmm,' was all Delaney said in reply, his thoughts running along the lines that he was bound to have had a hand in it, whatever.

Then, as he came close to the courthouse, he saw something that told him his thinking was right. Joey Sands came running out from behind it, a rifle in his hand and with a panicky look on his face.

'Stop!' Delaney called out to him.

Joey nearly died when he found himself coming almost face to face with the sheriff. It made him stop dead in his tracks.

'Where you going, Joey?' Delaney asked him.

But before Joey could reply Dick Arnold appeared at his rear with his gun drawn. For a moment all three men remained still, then Arnold called out to Joey to drop his rifle.

But Joey was in too much of a panic to give up so easily. Spotting an alley on his left he suddenly bolted and ran up it. Arnold somehow or other was not able yet to make himself take a shot at him. Instead, he went to give chase after him.

'Leave him to me,' Delaney ordered him.

Stopping in his tracks, Arnold replied in flamingly angry tones, 'He shot at Jimboy, Tom. Again, someone shot at one of my sons. Maybe it was him all along who shot Red.'

'Maybe, but I doubt it,' Delaney replied. 'But whatever, I'm the law round here, Dick, and you can't go taking it into your own hands.'

Arnold took in what the sheriff said and considered it for a moment but then decided he didn't care what the law was. They'd got away with it once but no one was going to get away with shooting at his family a second time. Without bothering to reply to what Delaney had said, he took off up the alley after Joey. Delaney followed. The alley was deserted, though, and Joey was no-where to be seen.

'Where are you, Joey? Come out now and fight like a man. I know it's you,' Arnold called out, his eyes darting from building to building and any cover they might be able to offer a fleeing man.

By now Sheriff Delaney was in the alley.

'Leave it, Dick,' he called out to Arnold. 'Otherwise I'm gonna have to arrest you.'

'Go away, Tom,' was Arnold's reply. 'This is my fight. Leave me to it.'

Delaney kept coming up the alley.

'I said stay away, Tom, and I mean it. The law's done nothing for Red. I don't aim to stand by and let it do nothing for Jimboy.'

There was a sudden movement in a doorway a few yards from Arnold. Without hesitating he let rip at it with his sixgun. Then another shot rang out and Dick Arnold was sent spinning around from the impact of a bullet that slammed into his chest.

'Oh God, no!' Delaney let out, his eyes

darting in all directions, scanning the two-storey building that loomed large around him.

'Joey, if that was you, come out now,' he called out after a few seconds.

Joey was hiding in the doorway of a back entrance to one of the buildings. He was feeling sick with what he'd done. He'd always liked Mr Arnold, as he respectfully thought of him, and didn't know why he'd shot him. But now he was consumed with fear of what he knew the consequences of having done so must surely be. Mr Arnold looked dead and that made him a murderer.

'I said come out, Joey,' Sheriff Delaney repeated. 'And with your hands up and your gun thrown out in front of you.'

Dick Arnold was not moving and by now Joey was almost a blubbering wreck. He might have given himself up to Delaney had not the alley suddenly filled with Cody Freeman, Pete Hammer and their gang, all with guns drawn, cocked, and fingers itching to pull the triggers. They were at the

Main Street end of the alley. Before a word could be uttered by anyone, Hal Turner and his gang appeared at the other end. Dick Arnold lying apparently dead on the ground, was visible to all. An eerie sort of stillness filled the air as for a few seconds they all simply took in what had appeared to have happened. From taking in the sight of Dick Arnold lying on the ground, their eyes shifted to look down the alley. Each group eyeballed the other.

Delaney knew, or reckoned he knew, why Hal Turner was there and whose side he would be on. But what had all this to do with Freeman and Hammer and their gang?

'All right,' he suddenly declared. 'I got this matter under control. Why don't you all just back off and leave me to do my job.'

Hal Turner might have obeyed him, but Freeman and Hammer had no intention of doing so.

'Where is he, Sheriff?' Freeman asked. 'The low-down son of a dog has gotta pay for what he did, no matter who he was doing it for and for why.'

The question panicked Joey and he decided he had to try and make a run for it. The door opposite where he was hiding was the back door of Mason's saloon. If he could only get to it, he reckoned he could make an escape through the saloon and, if he was lucky, get to a horse.

Before Delaney could answer Freeman's question, Joey came running out from where he was hiding, his gun blasting. As a precaution against its being locked, he was shooting at the handle of the saloon door. He had crashed through it before the others in the alley realized what was happening. But the sound of a gun firing prompted them all to open fire. Delaney would have been cut down where he stood had he not dived to the ground. Some of Freeman's gang were not so quick or lucky and fell to the ground.

'Go cover the front of Mason's,' Delaney ordered the gang of cowboys, collecting himself quickly. He'd realized he'd lost control of the situation, and that all he could do was enlist the help of those around him to try and get it back.

In Mason's saloon Bob Wills and his fiddle band were giving a rousing rendition of 'Turkey in the Straw' and a number of drunken cowboys had taken to the floor to dance a jig. What had happened some minutes before was not enough to spoil their fun. Nobody heard the shots Joey had fired and no one paid him much attention as he tried to push his way through the revellers. He'd have no doubt made good his escape, had not Freeman and Hammer, followed by their gang, suddenly come bursting through the saloon's batwing doors.

'Oh, oh,' Bob Wills thought to himself, on catching sight of Freeman and Hammer and their drawn guns. As was his wont though, he played on and with even more gusto than normal, letting go one of his characteristic 'ah-ah's'.

Freeman and Hammer knew who they

were looking for. Catching sight of him, and heedless of the fact that he was in the middle of a seething mass of humanity, they opened fire on him. The place erupted into chaos. Nevertheless Bob Wills didn't stop playing. But as bullets slammed home into some of their number, the dancers stopped their jigging and dived to the floor for cover. Joey turned and ran back the way he had come. While Freeman gave chase, Hammer ran back through the batwings, intending to catch Joey in the alley. He ran straight into the arms of Hal Turner and his gang. But while Turner and his gang were just delinquent kids playing at being tough, Peter Hammer was the real thing.

Before Turner knew what had happened, Hammer smashed him in the face with the butt of his Colt .45, sending him sprawling. His gang was similarly dealt with. Witnessing it happening was Red Arnold, who, on hearing gunfire and realizing there was a fight going on in town that might be involving his brother and his father, had got up from his sick-bed and, ignoring the complaints from his mother and Lucy, gone to investigate. The alley in which all the action had taken place was virtually opposite the doctor's surgery. Red stepped out just in time to see Sheriff Delaney dragging Joey out from the alley. Hot on Delaney's heels and flying at him was Cody Freeman. The three of them fell to the ground in a heap. As they wrestled one another, each trying to get the better of the others, a shot rang out. Then another. Undeterred, the three men carried on, kicking up the dust of Main Street.

'Stop!' shouted Peter Hammer. 'Before I fill the three of you with lead.'

Cody Freeman was the first to pull himself free from the tangle of bodies.

'OK, OK,' he snarled at his sidekick, 'no need to get so excited.'

As he spoke Freeman was going for his gun. Townsfolk and spectators of the bull-riding were gathering around and he wanted to make sure that if anyone took control of the situation it was going to be himself and Hammer and no one else.

'Put that gun away, cowboy,' Sheriff Delaney, who had quickly got to his feet, ordered Freeman.

He had again taken hold of Joey and had pulled him to his feet.

'Who's gonna make me, Sheriff? You?' Freeman asked, looking around him to indicate to Delaney that he, Hammer and their gang, all of whom had drawn and cocked their sixguns, were quite definitely in command of the situation.

'Yeah,' snarled Delaney, in between catching his breath. ''Cause contrary to what everyone seems to think I am the law round here.'

But even as he said it he knew it wouldn't carry much weight with the bunch of cowboys now confronting him. Still, he wasn't going to give them a chance to contradict him. He was about to turn away from them and take Joey to his office, when Red Arnold suddenly caught sight of his father lying apparently lifeless half-way up the alley.

'Pa!' he suddenly exclaimed, leaping from the boardwalk from where he'd watched what had been going on. 'Pa!'

Sheriff Delaney tried to say something to him but never got the chance. Red had got to his father's side in a flash. He arrived there just in time to witness his father begin to come round. To the others, though, it continued to look as if the shot Joey had fired at Dick Arnold had indeed killed him.

Realizing it was more imperative now than ever that he remove Joey to his office, Delaney began again to try and do so.

'You ain't taking him nowhere, Sheriff,' Freeman suddenly declared. 'At least not until he's paid the price for what he's done. So why don't you save us all a lot of trouble and just hand him over.'

Quite a crowd had gathered to witness what was going on and suddenly it became very quiet. It felt to all as if there was going to be a lynching. There were very few people in the crowd who didn't feel Joey deserved it.

'Now you know I can't do that,' Sheriff Delaney replied.

'Maybe you ain't got no choice in it,' Pete Hammer remarked.

Someone in the crowd called out 'let them have him' and soon everyone was indicating it was how they felt. Joey suddenly realized what Freeman was intending to do and he near filled his pants with fear.

'Hal,' he called to Turner pathetically, 'you ain't gonna let nobody hang me, are you?'

Turner didn't reply. Somehow all the fight and bravado had been knocked out of him.

'No one's gonna let you be hanged without a proper trial,' a voice called down from the roof of the saloon. It was Del Lawson, Henry Turner's foreman. 'Now drop your guns, all of you, before I drop *you*.'

Freeman just laughed. 'Don't this town just beat 'em all?' he joked, turning to Hammer.

'It sure do,' Hammer agreed.

Then quick as lightning he turned to look up at Lawson. Almost before Lawson had realized what was happening, lead spat up at him from Hammer's gun and ripped into his chest. He was dead before he landed in a heap at the feet of Hal Turner.

Sheriff Delaney looked on in horror. The odds were stacked too heavily against him and it showed in his demeanour. Freeman knew that if he acted quickly the day could be theirs. With his gun still drawn, he strode up to Joey and taking him by the front of his shirt pulled him out of Delaney's grip.

'Go get a horse and some rope,' he said to one of his gang.

Then, pushing Joey ahead of him, he began to walk in the direction of the court-house square. There were trees there and he intended to hang Joey from one of them. The crowd could see what his intentions were and fell in behind him. They began to talk amongst themselves about how they believed in natural justice and that Dick Arnold had been a good man and that he and his boys hadn't deserved what had happened to them.

Dick Arnold, though, was far from dead, which meant that Joey Sands was far from being a murderer. The bullet he'd shot at Dick Arnold had passed straight through him, somehow missing his vital organs and major arteries. Sure, he was in a bad way, but he wasn't dead. That this was so was soon made apparent to Red.

'Jimboy,' his father struggled to say to him, 'where is Jimboy?'

Red didn't know where his kid brother was but he knew it was best to humour his father.

'He's all right, Pa. Don't worry about him. He's all right.'

'That's all right, then, son,' Arnold replied. 'And Joey, what's happened to him?'

Red didn't know how to answer him. Then a realization suddenly dawned on him.

'Pa,' he asked. 'You're not saying it was Joey who shot you, are you?'

Arnold didn't answer him but he didn't need to. The expression on his face told all.

Red was stunned. He hadn't known before why Freeman and Hammer were determined to get their hands on Joey; now he could guess and it sent shivers running down his spine. Looking at his father, he didn't know what to do next.

'Joey's all right, too,' he said in a deeply abstracted way to his father.

'That's all right, then,' Arnold replied, before suddenly giving way to his injuries and lapsing into semi-consciousness.

Red realized he needed a doctor. He looked around for someone to help him, expecting still to see the crowd at the bottom of the alley. But there was no one there.

'I'm just going for help, Pa. You just lie there and don't move,' he said.

As he tried to leave, his father suddenly came to again and took hold of him by the shirt.

'You ain't lying about Joey?' he struggled to ask. 'He's still alive, ain't he?'

'Sheriff's got him,' was all Red said in reply.

'That's all right then,' his father remarked, letting go of his elder son's shirt and slipping back into semi-consciousness. But not before uttering, 'Just a boy, just a stupid, crazy boy.'

Choked by his father's goodness, Red ran up the alley in time to see the back of the crowd as it filled the courthouse square. Looking from them to Dr Ritchie's surgery and back again, he didn't know what to do for the best. Run after Freeman and the rest and tell them his father wasn't dead, and by so doing save Joey from a nasty death, or make straight for Dr Ritchie's surgery. Whose life should take priority? Of course he knew the answer. He turned and ran as fast as his legs and poor health would carry him.

'Looks pretty nasty out there,' Dr Ritchie remarked to him as he came bursting in through the surgery door.

'Pa's hurt,' he blurted out to him.

'What?' asked Dr Ritchie.

Sally Arnold was there. Her relief at seeing

Red return unharmed quickly turned to panic on hearing that her husband was not. She jumped to her feet and ran to him exclaiming, 'What do you mean, Red? Is he hurt bad?'

'He's been shot in the chest but he's alive and talking.'

'Take me to him,' Dr Ritchie demanded, taking hold of his medical bag. As Red led his mother and Dr Ritchie to where he'd left his father things were hotting up where Freeman and Hammer were getting ready to lynch Joey. By now Red was beginning to wonder where Jimboy was. As Dr Ritchie tended to his father and his mother fussed around him, he suddenly felt an urgency about letting Sheriff Delaney know that his father was not dead. His mother was about to ask him who it was who had shot his father, when he suddenly declared:

'It was Joey that did it and now they're fixing to hang him. I gotta go tell them Pa's not dead.'

A look of horror spread across both his

mother's and Dr Ritchie's faces.

'Do that, son,' Dr Ritchie said. 'Your pa's hurt bad but I think he's gonna be all right. We need to get him moved to the surgery. But you hurry off before something terrible is allowed to happen.'

'Did you say Joey did this?' Sally Arnold said, grabbing Red by the arm as he went to go.

With a nod of the head, he indicated that he had.

'But why?' his mother asked in bewildered tones.

'I don't know, Ma, I really don't know,' Red replied, giving his mother an anxious look. 'But I can't let him be lynched for it, can I?'

'Go,' she said. 'Go.'

He arrived on the scene of the planned lynching just in time to see Hammer and Freeman throwing Joey, whose hands were tied behind his back, up on a horse. Hal Turner and his gang, disarmed and looking broken, were standing nearby with the guns of Freeman's and Hammer's people trained on them.

'Pa ain't dead,' he announced at the top of his voice to the gathering. 'He's hurt bad but he ain't dead.'

A hum of voices questioning what they'd just heard issued from the crowd, while Sheriff Delaney pulled himself free from his captors and said in loud and authoritative tones, '*Now* will you stop this nonsense and let me take Joey and lock him up in the jail house?'

Freeman and Hammer looked at one another. They were not minded to do any such thing.

'Well, if your father is alive, and we've only your word for it, Joey here still tried to kill him, and your brother, don't forget that.'

'Yeah,' voices from the crowd began to call out. Their blood was up.

'I did not,' Joey declared. 'I was just trying to unseat him, that was all. I swear it.'

'Hang him anyway!' someone in the crowd was heard to cry, echoed by others.

'You ain't so innocent yourself,' Sheriff Delaney declared to Hammer, raising his voice above that of everyone else's to make sure he was heard. But it wasn't just Delaney who'd thought of this fact. The very same knowledge had begun to concentrate both Freeman's and Hammer's minds. Both men had indeed realized that if they began to give ground to Delaney they ran the risk of being arrested themselves for the murder of Del Lawson.

Anything might have happened next as the cowboys and Sheriff Delaney stood facing one another, getting ready to tough it out, had not Henry Turner and a dozen of his men suddenly come riding into their midst. Looking around, Henry Turner was relieved to see that his son was still alive. Seeing Joey astride a horse with his hands tied behind his back he knew he'd arrived not a minute too soon. If they were going to lynch Joey, would it have been long before they put a rope around Hal's neck, too?

'Sheriff Delaney, you part of this?' he

asked with the commanding tone of a big shot in the community.

'He's been trying to stop it,' Hal Turner offered up.

'Shut up, Hal!' Turner snapped at him. 'I was asking Sheriff Delaney, not you.'

Then, turning back to Delaney, he demanded to know what was going on and why. As the sheriff began to explain, Hammer and Freeman, sensing that for them the game was up, began again to apply their minds to saving their own skins. Looking at Hammer, Freeman gave him the nod and suddenly both of them flew into action. Flying at two of Turner's horsemen, they knocked them from their mounts, jumped up on them and began to make a getaway. They rode straight into the crowd, reckoning that neither Turner nor his men would open fire on them and risk hurting innocent people.

But they were wrong. Henry Turner was the first to spur his horse into action to chase after them. As he did so, he pulled a gun, firing at the fleeing cowboys over the heads of the crowd. He shouted over his shoulder to his men to follow. Soon they were all giving chase, firing madly as they went. Hammer and Freeman soon realized that the move they had made had not been so clever. If they carried on running their chances of survival were not going to be good. So, instead of continuing to ride hell for leather out of town, they reined in their horses, jumped off them and ran for cover down an alley, shooting behind them as they went. They were both crack shots and easily felled two of Turner's men. But the rest spread out around the mouth of the alley and kept up enough of a storm to keep Freeman and Hammer pinned down, one on either side of the alley. The two outlaws planned to run up the alley and escape over the railway tracks it led to.

'God damn it!' Freeman exclaimed as a shot came winging past him from what was to his mind the wrong direction.

He craned his neck to see where it was

coming from and caught sight of Hal Turner peering around the corner of a building at the far end of the alley.

'That little runt!' he thought to himself, cursing and blaming him for being the cause of the trouble he and Hammer were now in.

Without hesitating he let go a gun-chamber of slugs in his direction, showering him with splinters of wood.

'You see what I see?' he called over to Hammer, indicating with a tilt of his head the direction in which Hammer should look.

Hammer looked in time to see Hal Turner poke his head out again from behind the building at the end of the alley and fire a shot. Looking back at Freeman, he simply nodded. Both Hammer and Freeman looked all around them to see if there was anywhere else to use as an escape route, but could see no other obvious way out. Resigned to what they began to see was their fate, the two men kept up a barrage of gunfire.

The shoot-out went on for some time. Henry Turner and Sheriff Delaney began to consider giving Freeman and Hammer the chance to give themselves up.

'What d'you think?' Henry Turner asked Delaney.

Delaney indicated with a shrug of his shoulders that they might as well give it a try. Henry Turner ordered his men to cease fire. Then he called out to Freeman and Hammer, offering them the opportunity to give themselves up. But neither of the two cowboys was the giving-in type. It was no cut-and-dry matter to them that they had killed a man. Their experience of life in the Wild West had taught them it was a dog-eat-dog world. If they hadn't killed Lawson, most likely he'd have killed them, was how they saw it.

'Well?' Henry Turner called out to them after a few minutes' silence, which he reckoned had given them long enough to make up their minds.

A quick answer did not seem to be forthcoming. Red was amongst the men keeping Freeman and Hammer pinned down but he hadn't joined in the shooting. He knew that what had started all this was the two cowboys rushing to the defence of Jimboy and he reckoned he owed them something, whatever crazy notions of loyalty had lain behind their actions.

Making his way to Sheriff Delaney's side, he asked him, 'Sheriff, what's gonna happen to them if they give themselves up?'

'They'll hang,' Henry Turner answered for him.

'After a trial,' Delaney was quick to add, his tone of voice indicating that they'd avoided one lynching and he wasn't about to let another take place.

'Yes, but they was only reacting to Joey shooting the bull from under Jimboy.'

'By murdering my foreman,' remarked Henry Turner.

As he said it, Freeman gave him his own and Hammer's answer. He jumped out into the street, his sixgun blasting. As he did so,

Freeman in turn broke cover and made a run for the top end of the alley, not stopping until he reached the spot where Hal Turner was taking cover. Before Hal Turner knew what had happened, Freeman's gun was jammed up under his chin. Never did a man look more surprised to see his circumstances change in less than the twinkling of an eye than Turner did at that moment. Hal Turner, as far as trouble-making went, was an amateur; Freeman was the real thing.

'Now, you little shit, you're gonna do what I tell you or I'm gonna blow your pretty little head off!' Freeman snarled at him.

Turner looked to the few men of his gang who were with him to do something but none of them did. Freeman's sudden appearance amongst them turned them all to stone. Not paying them the least mind, Freeman turned to Turner and snarled, 'Right now, start walking.'

Before he had a chance to protest Turner found himself looking down the length of the alley, along which were still flying slugs of every calibre.

'Hold your fire, men!' a startled Henry Turner called out on seeing his son make his sudden appearance. 'Hold your fire, I say, all of you. That's Hal up there.'

'My God you're right,' Sheriff Delaney gasped. 'What's Freeman playing at?'

Henry Turner simply grimaced and tried to swallow on what had suddenly become a tight and dry throat. He knew very well what was going on, even if he wasn't prepared to let anyone see he was intimidated by it.

'Let him go,' he called out to Freeman.

Freeman, though, just sniggered the bad man's snigger. As he drew level with where Hal was again taking cover, Freeman stepped into the alley, cocking his gun as he did so and aiming it at Hal Turner's left temple. It so terrified him he had to fight not to soil his britches.

'All right,' Sheriff Delaney called out, stepping into the open. 'That's enough now. What do you want?'

'Two horses and a safe passage out of

town,' Freeman replied.

Delaney turned to Henry Turner to see what he thought.

'They can have their horses but they've gotta leave Hal behind,' was all he said.

There were a number of crack shots amongst his men and he was of a mind to try and create a situation whereby they would try and take out Freeman and Hammer but, no matter how much contempt he felt for his stupid arse son, he couldn't bring himself to take any chances with his life.

'Tell them,' he ordered Delaney.

'He goes with us,' was the stark and un-compromising reply that came back.

'Maybe I could talk to them,' offered Red, who hadn't left the scene, despite not wanting to join in the shooting.

'What good do you think that would do, boy?' Henry Turner asked him impatiently.

But before Red Arnold could reply something happened that startled all of them. Jimboy appeared at the top of the alley with a rifle. Red's stomach jumped to his mouth as he saw his kid brother putting himself in mortal danger. Neither Freeman nor Hammer were yet aware that Jimboy was there, but they were soon to find out.

'Let him go,' a boyish but determined voice called out to them.

Startled, they turned round to see who it was.

'You?' Hammer questioned out loud but barely loud enough to be heard.

'Don't be stupid, boy,' was all Freeman said. 'Either we ride out of here with this pile of shit or we all die here, right now.'

Hal Turner should have been relieved at what was happening, but the only bit about him that was relieved were his bowels. The stench was foul and it made both Freeman and Hammer step aside from him. Jimboy could see what had happened and it filled him with a great deal of satisfaction. It was going to be something Turner would never be able to live down.

'You're putting your neck on the line for *this?*' Freeman asked Jimboy.

Neither he nor Hammer had let their guard down, despite a strong desire to get as far away from Hal Turner as possible.

'Why don't we just kill him now?' Hammer asked.

'The youth in Pecos seem to present nothing but trouble,' Freeman suddenly declared, looking in the direction of the Main Street end of the alley and making it clear to everyone down there that his words were meant for them. 'Now we don't wanna kill Jimboy here, but looks like we might have to, unless'n of course one of you can talk sense to him. Now I'm gonna count to ten and then we're leaving this alley, one way or another.'

The scene was already pretty tense but as Freeman began to count it got tenser. He got to five before anyone answered.

'Jimboy, you're a brave young son of a gun, but I think this is something you gotta leave me and Hal's pa here to sort out,' Sheriff Delaney said at last.

Jimboy, however, did not appear to falter

in his determination to free Hal Turner from Freeman's and Hammer's clutches. And to his own way of thinking he had his reasons.

'Hal ain't going nowhere until he confesses to shooting Red. Make him do that and anyone can have him,' he replied, his hands clutching more firmly the rifle he was holding to his shoulder, his shooting-eye still keenly looking down the sights.

'Well?' Sheriff Delaney called out to Hal Turner. 'Was it you?'

Hal didn't seem inclined to reply and it incensed Freeman.

'Well, did ya?' he snarled at him. 'Did ya?' he asked again, raising his voice to fever pitch.

'Yes, yes, I did,' Turner blurted out, falling to his knees and feeling so humiliated he wanted to cry.

'All right, enough!' his father suddenly called out, stepping into the open. His gun was down. 'Let's end this whole thing now. You can have your horses and you can ride out of town and no one'll try and stop you.'

'How do we know you ain't bluffing?' Freeman asked him.

'Because I said so,' Henry Turner roared back at him. 'Now get out of town before I change my mind.'

While neither Freeman nor Hammer was the sort to be told what to do when they had a mind to do it their own way, they were quick to know a good thing when they saw it. Keeping their guns up and without saying another word, they slowly began to back down the alley, pushing past Jimboy, who did nothing to stop them, instead keeping his eyes fixed firmly on Hal Turner, who was still on his knees looking pathetically exposed.

Henry Turner watched Freeman and Hammer disappear from the end of the alley before reholstering his gun. Then wearily he turned to Sheriff Delaney and said, 'Do whatever the law has to do with him.'

So saying and without casting a look his son's way, he walked off, his men slowly falling into line behind him.

TWELVE

Dick Arnold lived and it wasn't long before he was back on his feet working his ranch. At Joey's trial he asked the judge to show Joey some leniency, but what he didn't know was that a deal had already been struck between Hal Turner's lawyer and the state prosecutor. Sheriff Delaney made sure that if money and influence was going to get Hal Turner off the hook, it was also going to benefit Joey. Trouble was Henry Turner wasn't that minded to give his delinquent son so easy a ride. But everyone agreed in the end it wasn't because he was criminally bad that Hal Turner caused all the trouble he did. It was just that he was, well, useless, useless as a .22 cartridge in a ten-gauge shotgun. His bad behaviour was just him trying to cover it up. Added to which, hadn't he been humiliated enough?

As for Cody Freeman and Pete Hammer, they got clean away but ended up going the way of all outlaws. Freeman was killed in a shoot-out with a card-player he tried to cheat; Hammer died a few years later at the end of a rope for cattle-stealing.

Jimboy would in time grow up to become Pecos's first great town marshal, going down in history as the man who made the town safe for ordinary, decent law-abiding folk to go about their daily business.

And bull-riding? Red Arnold won the Fourth of July bull-riding championships for the next decade in Pecos and every Fourth of July since. As the world enters the twenty-first century, The West of the Pecos Rodeo re-enacts the kind of events for which he became legendary.

The publishers hope that this book has given you enjoyable reading. Large Print Books are especially designed to be as easy to see and hold as possible. If you wish a complete list of our books please ask at your local library or write directly to:

Dales Large Print Books
Magna House, Long Preston,
Skipton, North Yorkshire.
BD23 4ND

This Large Print Book, for people
who cannot read normal print,
is published under the auspices of
THE ULVERSCROFT FOUNDATION